'Annie?' he said hoarsely.

Then Max looked again at the boy, so like his nephew it was uncanny, and knew with a shock that took his breath away that this beautiful, healthy, mischievous child was his son.

She wanted to run. She wanted to grab Harry and leg it, out of the shop, into the car, miles away where he couldn't find them. Anything rather than stand there and explain, in front of the shoppers, just what this man meant to her.

And so she did the only thing left open to her. She met his eyes, dragged in a deep breath and said, 'Hello, Max.'

Caroline Anderson's nursing career was brought to an abrupt halt by a back injury, but her interest in medical things led her to work first as a medical secretary and then, after completing her teacher training, as a lecturer in Medical Office Practice to trainee medical secretaries. She lives in rural Suffolk with her husband, two daughters and assorted animals.

Recent titles by the same author:

THE GIRL NEXT DOOR
PRACTICALLY PERFECT

MAKING MEMORIES

BY
CAROLINE ANDERSON

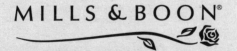

For Trisha, with love.

*First published in Great Britain 2000
Harlequin Mills & Boon Limited,
Eton House, 18-24 Paradise Road, Richmond, Surrey TW9 1SR*

© Caroline Anderson 2000

ISBN 0 263 82251 6

*Set in Times Roman 10½ on 12 pt.
03-0008-48402*

*Printed and bound in Spain
by Litografia Rosés, S.A., Barcelona*

CHAPTER ONE

THE little shop was busy. It was good, Max thought, to see such support for a tiny rural supermarket. It implied a thriving community—not that he would be part of it for long. He wasn't part of anything for long these days.

Stifling a pang of regret, he went in, grabbed a basket and threw in a few basic essentials. Bread, butter, milk, cheese, tomatoes, a local paper, marmalade for breakfast, and biscuits for late-night snacking. Chocolate biscuits, for a change, a housewarming present to himself.

He gave a wry snort, went round the corner of the aisle and tripped over something small and soft and indignant.

His basket went flying, he crashed into the magazine stand and scattered the contents wildly. Muttering a quiet oath, he bent and scooped up an armful of machine knitting patterns and gardening periodicals, then lifted his eyes to see what he'd fallen over and met the worried gaze of a small boy.

Good grief, he was so like his nephew! All eyes, lurking with mischief and now distinctly worried—because he had been playing with a toy car in the middle of the aisle when Max had fallen over him.

He smiled, and the child gave him a tentative smile in return. 'Oops,' Max said in a conspiratorial stage whisper, and the boy giggled. Had they got away with it?

'Are you all right?' he asked, and the boy nodded.

'I banged my hand.'

'I'm sorry. I wasn't looking.'

He stood up, dusting off his grubby little knees. ''S OK. Doesn't hurt.'

Max put the magazines back, grabbed his basket and looked up, just as a young woman came round the corner.

'Harry? Are you all right?'

She bent down, her hair falling over her face, and Max's heart jolted.

Don't be a fool, he told himself in disgust. You think every woman between twenty and fifty looks like her.

And then she stood up, and he felt the colour drain from his cheeks. He straightened, the basket dangling forgotten at his side, his eyes locked with hers.

'Annie?' he said hoarsely, and then he looked again at the boy, so like his nephew it was uncanny, and knew with a shock that took his breath away that this beautiful, healthy, mischievous child was his son.

Annie wanted to run. She wanted to grab Harry and leg it, out of the shop, into the car, miles away where he couldn't find them. Anything rather than stand there and explain, in front of Mrs Bootle and the rest of her cronies, just what this man meant to her.

And so she did the only thing left open to her. She met his eyes, dragged in a deep breath and said, 'Hello, Max.'

He looked hardly any different, she thought absently. Older, of course, but weren't they all? Harry had been a mere embryo the last time he'd been in the vicinity of his father. Scarcely that. In fact, Max's contribution to his son had probably still been swimming at the time.

Anna dragged Harry to his feet.

'Excuse us. We have a lot to do.' She turned, heading for the door, and Mrs Bootle's voice followed her.

'Don't forget your shopping, Anna!'

Muttering words Harry didn't know about under her breath, she turned back to the checkout, snatched up her carrier bag and made for the door again, her son trailing behind her.

A shadow fell across her path, and her way was suddenly blocked.

'I think we have some catching up to do,' he said in a soft voice that still sent shivers down her spine.

Did he know? Had he realised about Harry, or was he talking about them? It didn't matter. Either way, she wasn't talking—not after what he'd done to her.

She forced herself to meet his eyes—startling eyes, denim blue eyes that matched the jeans he was wearing and found an echo in her son's own eyes. She thought they were the most beautiful eyes she'd ever seen— and she'd hoped never to see them again.

'I don't think so,' she replied frostily. 'I can't think of a single thing I want to say to you that wouldn't consign me straight to hell. Please, move out of my way.'

He hesitated, his eyes so like Harry's searching hers, and deep within them she thought she saw a flicker of something that could have been pain.

Then he moved, stepping aside to let her pass, and she felt his eyes on her back all the way across the square, until she rounded the corner out of sight.

She let out her breath in a ragged sigh, and suddenly became aware of Harry, tugging her hand.

'You're hurting me,' he said petulantly, and she realised she had his wrist in a death-like grip.

She released it, crouching down and smoothing back his dark blond hair, another legacy from his father. 'Sorry, darling. I forgot what I was doing.' She hesitated, looking up her front path just feet away. She had an idea. 'Shall we go and see if Grannie's in?'

Harry started to whinge, a sure sign that he was tired after a busy day at nursery school, and Anna realised with resignation that she was going to have to go home and couldn't escape.

However, she felt strangely reluctant. It was almost as if she could still feel Max's eyes on her, watching her, following her.

She turned, scanning the edge of the square, but there was no one to be seen. At least, no one like him, tall, broad, dressed in denim jeans and a cool chambray shirt, with sun-tipped hair and eyes that could caress at one minute and cut holes in steel in the next.

She slipped her key into the lock, went through the door and closed it softly behind them. The cat ran to greet them, trotting down the stairs with a staccato 'Mreouw!'. Harry scooped him up.

'Want some juice and a biscuit?' she offered her son's departing back, and Harry nodded as he sauntered towards the sitting room.

'Two,' he said.

'One.'

'Two.'

Seconds later the television was on, and she trailed into the kitchen with her shopping, put the kettle on and sank down at the table, her head in her hands.

Max Carter was in town—and she was in big trouble, unless he decided to go quietly away and leave them in peace.

Somehow she doubted it, and the very thought sent shivers up her spine. Almost five years, she thought numbly. Five years without a word, without a murmur, and then he turns up out of the blue, on the other side of the country.

She tried to remember if she'd told him where her parents lived, but she didn't think so. They hadn't talked much. Their relationship had been wild and wicked and based on instinct and had lasted a grand total of three weeks. She'd given her heart to him, and he'd absconded with it, leaving her pregnant and alone. There had been little time for niceties of social exchange.

So what on earth was he doing here, in Wenham Market?

Causing trouble, that was a sure bet. It was one thing Max Carter did as easily as breathing.

And Anna's life would never be the same again.

It got worse. She hadn't imagined it could, of course, but, then, she'd reckoned without the tinkering and mischievous hand of fate.

He was working at the practice, as a locum.

Terrific. She'd be thrust into his company umpteen times a day, forced to work with him whether she liked it or not, and her only consolation was that it was a distinctly temporary post until Suzanna had had her baby and came back to work.

He was in a meeting with the other doctors, fortunately, and so she grabbed a cup of coffee, picked up a handful of notes and went into her treatment room. She could hide, at least, until later.

Her first patient—fate muscling in on the act, again—was one of Suzanna's, a man with a history of slight chest pain. Just her luck, the trace was abnormal, and so she had to take it in to Max immediately.

She debated seeing one of the other doctors, but that wasn't fair to them. With a resigned sigh she knocked on his door and popped her head round.

'Excuse me, Dr Carter—could I have a word?'

He gave her an unreadable look, stood up and stepped outside the door, pulling it to.

'On Friday you wouldn't talk to me,' he reminded her, his voice deadly quiet and edged with reproach.

'Today I have to,' she said acidly, thrusting the notes and the trace at him. 'Mr Jenks—history of mild intermittent chest pain. I thought you ought to see his ECG.'

He scanned it and frowned. 'I'd better see him—can you ask him to get himself fitted in?'

'Sure.' She turned on her heel and walked away, conscious of the holes seeming to burn in the back of her shoulders as he watched her. She went round the corner of the corridor, sagged against the wall and drew a deep breath.

Her knees felt like jelly, her heart was pounding and she'd lay odds her ECG trace would be highly abnormal as well. Darn the man! How *dare* he turn up and throw her life into confusion?

She shrugged away from the wall, opened the door of her treatment room and went in.

'Hello, Mr Jenks,' she said with a smile. 'I've spoken to Dr Carter, who's taken over from Dr Korrel while she's on maternity leave, and he'll see you shortly. If you ask at Reception, they'll give you a number and fit you in, so you can chat over the result with him—all right?'

He nodded and stood up, looking thoughtful. 'Bad, is it?' he asked.

'I'm not a doctor,' she told him honestly, avoiding answering the question directly. 'He'll go through the trace with you and explain it and set your mind at rest, I'm sure.'

'All right, thank you, Sister,' Mr Jenks said, and went out to arrange his appointment.

Absently Anna unrolled clean paper onto the couch, tore off the used section and put it in the bin, and tidied up the ECG machine. Should she have told him more? Probably not. She didn't know how Max would handle it, or if he'd refer him to a cardiologist. It wasn't her place to discuss the result with patients, just to do the test and pass it all on.

Nevertheless, he'd been right—it was bad. Worse than his symptoms indicated.

She sighed, picked up the notes of the next patient and pressed the call button that buzzed and flashed a light by her name in the waiting room. Max could deal with Mr Jenks. That was why he was there, and he may as well earn his keep.

The morning went. That was all she could say about it. It didn't drag, but it didn't fly, and the whole time she was conscious of the presence, just round the corner, of the man who single-handedly had altered the entire course of her life.

Her last patient dealt with, and nothing left to do in her room, no further reason she could find to hide, she went back out to the office and bumped straight into him.

Blast. She'd hoped he would still be doing a surgery, but no such luck. She glared at him, just as he lifted his head and met her eyes, and then he smiled at her, a twisted, wry smile, and her whole world tipped up-side down.

How could she still feel like this about him? After the way he'd walked out, how could she possibly still fall for that lazy, sexy, wicked mouth and those stunning baby blues?

She just wanted to flee, but it wasn't going to be that easy. David Fellows, the senior partner, put his arm round her shoulders and cut off her escape. 'Ah, Anna,' he boomed in his patronising and slightly irritating manner. 'Come and meet our locum, Max Carter. Max, this is Anna Young, one of our highly valuable and skilled team of practice nurses.'

'We've met,' they said in unison. Max's voice was quiet, matter-of-fact. Hers was—oh, Lord, bitter. He was turning her into a shrew, and she wasn't like that. Tears stung her eyes and she turned away, heading for the sanctuary of her room again, but she couldn't stay in there all day and she knew it. She went home for lunch, ignoring the deep, slightly gruff voice that called her name, and headed across the square and round the corner with her head down.

He followed her, of course, arriving at her front door almost as she did, so she had no opportunity to slip inside and shut it in his face.

Instead, she turned on him. 'What do you want with me?' she asked, a touch of frenzy in her voice. She steadied herself with a huge effort. 'Why are you here? What do you want?'

'You know why I'm here—covering for Suzanna Korrel. As to what I want...' He reached out and lifted a tendril of hair which had escaped from her braid, and twirled it idly around his finger. His eyes locked with hers, the message clear, sending shivers of dreadful anticipation through her traitorous body. 'I'd like to know about my son.'

His son? Anna closed her eyes, an icy chill washing over her. So he did know. And very likely, then, had tracked her down.

'What makes you think he's your son?' she asked, clutching at straws.

'The fact that he has my eyes? My father's eyes? My brother's eyes? My nephew's eyes? He's the right sort of age, he looks like me—I would think that's pretty conclusive.'

She turned, opened the door and went in. 'You lost all rights to know him when you walked out on me,' she told him bluntly. 'As far as I'm concerned, he's *my* son, and he doesn't have a father.'

She pushed the door to, but it wouldn't close. A large well-polished masculine shoe was stuck in the crack. She debated slamming the door hard against it to crush it, but thought it more likely that the door would break.

She dropped her forehead against the wood and sighed. 'Please, Max, leave me alone,' she pleaded wearily. 'You can't just waltz back into my life after five years and expect to be welcomed with open arms. Now get your foot out of the door and go!'

Her voice cracked on the last word, and after a second the shoe disappeared. 'I'm sorry, Annie,' he said softly, and then the door closed quietly and she heard the slow, measured stride of his retreat.

Tears scalded her eyes and spilt down on the floor, her head in her hands, the cat rubbing self-indulgently against her shin. He'd just sounded so—what? Forlorn? Penitent? Hopeless?

She sighed thoughtfully. That didn't gel with her reasons for his arrival in her life. Was it possible she was wrong? Was he here just by coincidence?

Or was he just apologising because he wasn't going to let it rest? Because he had no intention of leaving her alone, and wanted his son?

Panic washed over her. What if he wanted to take Harry? What if he decided to go for custody? Or, worse still, kidnap him?

Terror gripped her, and she struggled to her feet and picked up the phone with trembling hands. She rang the nursery school, and was told Harry had gone home with his grandmother, as usual.

She sighed with relief, and told them that under no circumstances was Harry to leave the school with anyone except her or her mother, even with written permission.

'His father has turned up in our lives,' she explained to Carol, the young woman in charge of the school. She hated doing this but was so worried for Harry's safety that she felt she had no choice.

'What does he look like? What's his name?' Carol asked, and Anna hesitated. He was going to be part of the community for some months. Was it fair to him—or her—to discuss this painful secret?

'Max Carter,' she said eventually. 'He's...' How could she describe him? 'He's just like Harry,' she told her. 'Fair hair, blond streaks, bright blue eyes...' Sexy mouth, sinful black lashes, crooked grin calculated to decimate the defences of the most hardened man-hater.

Stick to the facts, she thought. 'About six foot, lean build—perhaps a little on the thin side,' she said, and realised with a jolt of surprise that he'd lost weight. 'Carol, don't say anything,' she added hastily. 'I don't want it getting out, and Harry doesn't know anything about him.'

'OK. Look, are you all right?'

She nodded, then remembered Carol couldn't see her. 'Yes, I'm fine,' she lied. 'I must go, I have to ring my mother.'

She pressed the cut-off button on the phone, dialled her mother and waited. It rang twice, then there was a clatter, and a little, high-pitched voice came over the phone. 'H'llo?'

She couldn't help the smile of relief. 'Hello, Harry, it's Mummy. Is Grannie there, darling?'

'Yup—Grannie!'

She held the phone away from her ear, rubbed it ruefully and switched sides. 'Mum?'

'Hello, darling. Everything all right?'

She suppressed the urge to laugh hysterically. 'Not really. I don't have time to explain, but watch Harry, OK? Don't let him out of your sight, and don't let anybody take him anywhere, no matter how plausible.'

There was a long silence, then her mother sighed softly. 'I take it he's turned up?'

Bless her. She never had to explain anything to her mother. 'Yes. I'll talk later. I have to grab some lunch and go back to work. Love you.'

Lunch was a piece of burnt toast which had got jammed in the toaster, a mouthful of cheese and a raspberry and blackberry yoghurt—always the last to go because she hated the seeds getting stuck in her teeth and Harry, predictably, had had the last strawberry one.

She had a glass of water because there wasn't time to make tea, and headed back across the square to the practice.

Max was sitting outside on the bench in the sun,

eating chips out of the wrapper and chatting to an elderly man, one of her less savoury regulars.

'Hello, Sister. You keepin' well?' Fred asked with his singsong, wheezy crackle.

'Fine, thank you, Fred. Yourself?'

'Oi'll do. Oi was just tellin' young Dr Car'er 'ere about my gout. Tha's got so much worse recently—'

'And it's nothing to do with all the booze, of course, is it?' she teased.

He looked shocked and pained. 'Oi ha'n't had a drop in weeks!' he protested, but Anna wasn't fooled.

'Pull the other, Fred. Mrs Bootle told me on Friday that you'd just been in for another bottle of cooking sherry.'

He scowled at her. 'Interferin' old trout,' he grumbled. 'I was going to make a trifle. She ain't got no business spreadin' malicious rumours 'bout me, shrivelled old bag.'

Anna laughed. 'I'm sure she loves you, too, Fred.' She went into the surgery, proud with herself for not once meeting Max's eye during that whole exchange, and made her preparations for the antenatal clinic.

Then a hideous thought struck her.

Suzanna always did the antenatal clinic on Mondays.

And Max was Suzanna's locum…

There was something strangely ordinary about working with Max. Both professionals in their own field, they just got on with the job and worked alongside each other without a hiccup.

How odd, when inside she was seething with doubts and fears and insecurities. Still, as long as he was in his consulting room with a patient he wasn't trying to abscond with Harry, which gave her a small element of comfort in the midst of her confusion.

Not that she thought he really would, but she'd only known him for such a short time, and now he was back in her life without warning, and wanted to talk. About custody?

She realised she wouldn't know what he was doing unless she talked to him—and that thought filled her with so many emotions she didn't know what way to turn.

Max wondered how he was going to be able to concentrate on his antenatal patients with Anna moving quietly around nearby, checking weights and testing urine and taking blood pressure, while he checked the lie of the baby and chatted to the mothers about their problems.

He'd wondered if any of them would object to having a man taking the clinic when they'd been used to Suzanna, but there didn't seem to be any adverse reaction. In fact, it was probably going to turn into the most enjoyable part of the week, he thought wryly. At least the women were there because they were well, and not because they were sick.

That made a refreshing change to the usual run of surgery time.

He caught sight of Anna through the open door as his patient left, and his gut clenched. Her hair was back in order, severely subdued by the French plait, with lighter strands at the front where the sun had caught it, setting off the smooth, clear skin and bright eyes.

She was lovely. Not fat, not thin, with curves in all the right places and a supple grace that he remembered well…

He groaned softly and pressed the buzzer for his next patient. He couldn't allow himself to think about her like that. Not now. Not with little Harry in the wings.

Maybe never.

'Annie?'

'It's Anna.'

He sighed quietly and leant against the wall by the back door of the practice. She'd come outside with her tea, and he'd followed her. Typical. Now she'd have to scald herself drinking it and go back inside.

'Don't run away. I only want to talk.'

'Well, I don't,' she said flatly, throwing her hot tea over a rose bush with a twinge of guilt. She pushed past him, irritated by the shiver of awareness that skimmed through her at the slight contact.

'Later, then.'

'Try when hell freezes,' she muttered under her breath, and went back to her room. She had a few patients in for routine checks, and then she could collect Harry and go home. It was none too soon.

'What does he want?'

Anna shrugged, and trailed a spoon over the top of her tea, bursting the little bubbles. 'He wants to know about Harry,' she said quietly, but her voice was vibrating with emotion. 'He thinks he can just breeze back into my life, persecute me at work and hound me at home.'

'What makes you think he even knows about Harry?' her mother asked.

'Because they've met—he fell over him, in the shop! He could hardly fail to notice him, and then I picked Harry up, and he looked at us—of course he's made the connection, and, anyway, he's told me he wants to know about his son. Trust me, Mum, he knows. Even if he didn't know before he arrived in Wenham Market, he knows now—and he wants to know more.'

Her mother shrugged philosophically. 'Why don't you talk to him, then? Get it over with—show him the photos, the videos of the birthday parties, the little clay things he's made. Bore him to death with the Mother's Day cards and the drawings and the pasta pictures—'

'I don't want to!' she said vehemently. 'It's nothing to do with him! None of it's anything to do with him!'

'Except that Harry is his son.'

She glared at her mother. 'Harry is the biological fruit of his loins, mother. He is *not* his son!'

One eloquent eyebrow arched expressively. 'Strikes me it's one and the same thing. You lost touch. Now he's back—'

'And what if he wants custody? What if he tries to take him from me?' she asked, desperation clawing at her.

Sarah Young tutted reproachfully. 'There isn't a judge in the land who would give him custody—don't be absurd. Is he married?'

'Married?' she echoed incredulously. How odd. She hadn't even given it a thought! 'I don't know,' she murmured. 'He didn't say.'

Her mother took the teaspoon away from her and patted her hand. 'Stop playing with your tea and drink it. Max isn't going to do anything. All he wants to do is talk.'

Anna sighed. 'I wish I could believe you, but I don't know him. I know hardly anything about him. He was a moment of foolishness, Mum, and I have no idea what kind of man he is or what he wants. All I know is that he walked out on me without any kind of explanation, and now he's back and I can't trust him. He could do anything—anything at all.'

She met her mother's eyes. 'Are you busy tonight? Could we stay for supper?'

'Because he knows where you live?'

She looked away. 'You think I'm being silly, don't you?' she said in a soft voice.

'I think you aren't giving him time to explain what he wants. I think that's a little unfair—'

'Unfair? *Unfair!* After what he did to me?' She pushed her tea away and stood up. 'I give up. You clearly don't want to see it from my viewpoint. You can't see how scared I am that I'll lose Harry—'

'You won't lose Harry—'

'I will if he kidnaps him,' she said flatly, and turned away, staring out of the window, her arms wrapped round her waist, hugging herself.

The words hung in the air.

Max sat on the front door step for ages. She'd left the surgery before him, and wasn't home. At least, if she was home, she wasn't answering her bell. Still, it was a pleasant summer evening. He'd gone home and changed into something more relaxed, because he'd thought he'd go for a walk, get to know the neighbourhood.

And he'd ended up here, waiting. Ridiculous. He'd start attracting attention, and then she'd get mad with him. That wouldn't help at all.

He stood up, just as the next-door neighbour came out of her house. 'She's not back yet—I expect she's at her parents'. Can I take a message?'

He smiled and leant over the honeysuckle hedge, his hand extended. 'Hello. I'm Dr Carter—I work with her.

I've taken over from Dr Korrel while she's on maternity leave. I just wanted a quick word.'

The neighbour shook his hand and moved closer, relaxing her guard. 'Jill Fraser. Dr Korrel's my doctor—I expect I'll be seeing you with one of my brood in the not-too-distant future, if our track record holds.'

She looked down the road. 'Why don't you go over to her mother's? They often stay late. I'm sure she won't mind, if it's important. It's the big Georgian house on the left, after all the other houses. There's a field, and then it's set back. Painted white—you can't miss it.'

He thanked her, and set off down the road, enjoying the feel of the sun on his face and the scented air. People were pottering in their gardens, watering hanging baskets and pots and tubs, tweaking weeds, picking roses. It was peaceful and domesticated and he envied them.

They smiled at him, said 'Lovely evening!' and things like that, and one or two recognised him and stopped him for a chat.

Then the houses petered out, and the lane narrowed, and then on the left, after a field full of fluffy, grazing sheep, was the house he was looking for.

It was a pretty house, not huge, but fairly substantial, the proportions elegant, the front garden deep with a gravelled turning circle in front of the house. He crunched over the gravel, rang the doorbell and waited.

A dog barked and was shushed, and then he heard the scrape of a key in the lock and the door swung inwards, revealing a softer, more mature version of Anna—the sort of woman his Anna would turn into given another twenty years. It was a pleasing thought.

'Mrs Young?'

She looked at him, searching his eyes. He obviously passed some sort of test, because she extended her hand. 'Sarah—and you must be Max,' she said calmly. 'Come on in. Anna's in the kitchen. We were just about to sit down to supper—why don't you join us?'

CHAPTER TWO

ANNA couldn't believe her ears. She'd eavesdropped blatantly at the kitchen door, worried that it might be Max, that he might have followed her here, and her mother was letting him in! *For supper!*

Sarah, indeed. She slammed the cutlery down on the table and turned to face the door, uncaring that hostility blazed from her usually gentle grey eyes. 'What the hell do you think you're doing here?' she snarled furiously. 'How *dare* you—?'

'Anna! Max is my guest, and you will treat him with respect—'

'What, like he treated me with respect? He walked out on me when I was pregnant—or have you conveniently forgotten that?'

Max intervened, a pained look on his face. 'At the time I had no idea—'

'And you didn't hang around long enough to find out, did you? Tell me—how many other times have you done this, Max? How many other little bastards are there wandering the streets, with your blue eyes and sexy smile?'

'Was that a compliment?' he asked wryly.

Sarah chipped in. 'Could we, please, discuss this rationally?' she pleaded.

'There's nothing to discuss. I'm leaving. Where's Harry?'

'Out checking sheep with your father. Anna, darling, sit down. Let Max have his say—ah, there they are now. George, come in. We've got a visitor—Max Carter.'

The name meant nothing to her father, but his face stopped George Young in his tracks. Years of diplomacy, however, prevented him reacting with anything but dignity. He nodded his head. 'Max. With you in a minute—Harry and I need to clean up a little bit. Come on, son, let's wash these hands.'

He hoisted the child up to the sink, propped him against the edge with his body and leant over him, soaping and rinsing until all four hands were clean. Then they dried them, and Harry turned and looked up at Max.

'You fell over me,' he said, recognising him for the first time. 'I got a bruise.'

'So've I,' Max said wryly, watching him with a painful intensity.

Anna glared at him. 'Don't you dare say *anything*,' she muttered under her breath for Max's ears alone.

He turned to her, his eyes curiously gentle. 'Don't worry, Anna,' he said softly. 'I'm not here to make trouble.'

It seemed he wasn't. He was charm itself, smiling and laughing at Harry's stories, engaging him in conversation and hanging on his every word.

And Harry adored him.

At least, he enjoyed the attention, and Anna kept trying to catch Max's eye to get him to cool it, but he assiduously avoided her attempts. It infuriated her, but she was helpless to say anything without triggering Harry's abundant curiosity, and so she sat there, and watched father and son together, and a great wave of regret and sadness washed over her for all the might-have-beens that Max had thrown away when he'd left her.

Then finally the meal was over, and Harry dragged Max into the sitting room to meet the dogs while Sarah made coffee. Anna followed with her father, unwilling to leave them alone together for as much as a second.

'Harry, go and ask Grannie if she can find that box of chocolates, would you, son?' George suggested, and Harry took off like a rocket. Her father dropped into his favourite chair with a slight groan, and stretched his legs.

'So, Max, what have you been doing for the past five years?' he asked cordially, settling back in his chair.

Anna held her breath. Was he married? Divorced? Widowed, even?

'Nothing terribly exciting,' Max said in a strangely calm voice. He was fondling the ears of one of the dogs, who was propped against his leg like a faithless hussy, grinning. 'I've done locum work in several practices—done some training courses in surgery and obstetrics, that sort of thing.'

'Never thought of settling down?'

Something flickered in his eyes, but then he leant back in the corner of the settee and gave a lazy smile. 'Maybe one day,' he said easily. 'For now I'm quite happy with variety.'

'And no responsibility,' Anna said under her breath.

'I have responsibilities,' Max corrected. 'Every patient that I see is my responsibility. What I don't have is ties.'

'And where does Harry fit into the great scheme of things?' she asked rashly, watching the door in case Harry came back in.

Max hesitated, something like regret flickering over his face. 'I don't know. I'd like to see him, obviously, but I don't think it's necessary for him to know exactly who I am. I would like to contribute towards his upbringing, though.'

'Conscience money?' Anna said bitterly.

Her father stood up and left the room, closing the door quietly behind him, and Max sighed and ran his hand through his hair.

'Annie, I don't want to fight with you. I didn't know I had a son until last Friday. I'm still feeling stunned. I'd like to know about him—about his birth, his early years, his first steps…' His voice was suddenly gruff, and he looked down at the dog, still patiently waiting for more attention. He tickled her ears again.

'I don't want you to feel threatened,' he went on after a moment. 'I can't take any real part in his life, for all sorts of reasons, but I would like to help you out with money, and I'd like to keep in touch and know how he's doing and what he's up to—that sort of thing.'

'So you want all the cream and none of the hard work, is that it?' she said, perversely furious that he didn't want to be involved in Harry's life.

'The cream?' he said with a trace of sadness. 'Is that what you call it? Knowing I have a son who doesn't know me, who will never know me as his father? Never know the joy of sharing his successes and the pain of standing back and letting him fail, if that's what's needed? Never sharing those special times, those late-night cuddles and quiet chats? You call that the cream?' He gave a humourless laugh. 'I would call that the crumbs from the table, Annie, but I know it's all I can have.'

'It's more than you deserve.'

He regarded her steadily. 'That's as may be. Whatever, will you allow me that? Will you tell me about him, share those early days and years with me, keep me in touch?'

'And in return you'll pay me to look after him. Is that it?'

He sighed shortly and stabbed his hands through his hair. 'I would contribute to his expenses whether you kept me in touch or not. It would just be nice to know how he's getting on.'

She let out her breath on a shaky sigh and stood up. 'I don't know. I'll show you pictures, tell you about him, but as for keeping in touch over the years—I don't know if I can do that. You hurt me, Max. I gave you everything I had to give, and you walked away. I don't know if I can face having you in my life again.'

He bowed his head. 'I'm sorry. You will never know how sorry I am.'

She snorted and walked to the door. 'I think it's time you went. I have to take Harry home and get him to bed. He can't have too many late nights during the week, he gets crabby and disgusting.'

'Like his mother,' Max said softly. 'You never were a morning person, were you, sweetheart?'

She stiffened at the endearment. 'Don't call me sweetheart. You lost all rights to call me that when you walked out. I'll tell you about your son, I'll share what I can of him with you while you're here, but that's all. No starting up where we left off, no thinking that you can use me and leave again. I won't have it. Do you understand?'

He stood up, crossing to stand behind her at the

doorway. 'I understand, Annie. Probably more than you realise. And I'm sorry.'

He moved past her and went down the hall to the front door. 'Thank your mother for supper for me, please. It was very kind of her.'

And he let himself out of the door, leaving her standing in the hall, her mind in a turmoil. Could she cope with him? With being so near him, talking to him, sharing Harry's early moments?

Remembering the things she'd had to do alone, when he should have been there to share them with her?

The thought filled her with dread, but underneath it was a strand of hope, a useless, optimistic thread of anticipation and excitement.

No, she told herself sternly. You don't want anything to do with him.

Even if he is the only man you've ever loved…

It was typical of fate's little tricks that she was scheduled the following day for minor surgery with Max. Just what I need, she thought, being stuck in the same room as him working alongside him for hours!

Still, it could have been worse. There were only three patients, and the first was a relatively simple incision of a cyst. Despite her best attempt at detachment, she was nevertheless interested to see how well and how carefully he worked. He really did have skill, she realised, and wondered again why he was still working as a locum instead of settling down somewhere in a permanent post.

Except, of course, that would give him ties, she thought bitterly. It still rankled that he didn't want to be part of Harry's life, and she conveniently forgot that just a short while before she'd been paranoid about him going for custody.

She forced herself to concentrate on their patient, and after Max had finished and stitched the little wound, she dressed it, cleaned up the little theatre and prepared it for the next patient.

'This one might be interesting,' Max said. 'A discharging sinus on a farmer's finger. He has a little shard of metal in it from an accident with machinery. It apparently healed and has now started swelling and discharging years later.'

'Is that Mr Bryant?' she asked, something prickling at the back of her mind.

'That's right. Why? Know him?'

'He's a friend of my father's. They farm next to us. I remember him doing it—a flywheel shattered and took off one of his fingers. This must be one of the ones that's left. Right, we're ready for him. Shall I go and get him?'

Max nodded, studying the notes. 'Please.'

She came back with Mr Bryant moments later, and Max shook his hand and introduced himself. 'Right, could we have a look at the offending digit?' he said with a smile.

'Sure. Here it is—I wouldn't have bothered, but every now and then it gets sore and infected, and, to be honest, Doc, it's a darned nuisance.'

He held out his hand, and Anna could see the great lump on the side of the tip of his finger. Half of the nail was missing, presumably lost in the original injury, and in the centre of the swelling was a nasty little black pit. Max pressed it gently, and it oozed.

'Right. Well, that looks straightforward enough. I've had a look at the X-ray, and it seems to be just one piece of metal—here, can you see?' He pointed the tiny fragment out on the X-ray, up on the light-box on the wall. 'All we have to do is find it.'

Mr Bryant laughed. 'Hope you've got good eyesight, Doc.'

'Twenty-twenty,' he assured him, then said softly under his breath, 'especially my hindsight.'

'What was that?' Mr Bryant said, looking puzzled.

'I said I have special eyesight,' Max lied blithely, and injected the finger to numb it, before scrubbing and gowning in preparation for the operation.

Anna laid out the trolley, taking care with aseptic technique so as not to contaminate any of the sterile packs, and by the time the finger was numb they were all ready.

The little shard of metal proved surprisingly elusive, but after a few moments Max found it and produced it with a flourish, like a conjurer with a rabbit.

'Right. That's the little blighter. Now all we need to do is clean up, and it should heal nicely all by itself. I'm not going to stitch it—this sort of thing needs to heal from the inside out. I'll ask Sister Young to dress it for you, and you'll need to come in and have the dressing changed every day for a week. By then it should be just about sorted. OK?'

'Excellent. Thank you, Doc. Lovely job.'

Anna attended to the wound, all the time chattering to him about farming and how her father was and the price of lambs at the market and the state of the industry, and by the time he left Max was staring at her in amazement.

'What?' she said crossly. 'Don't you dare tell me I gossip.'

He laughed. 'I was just stunned by your social skills.

You tell old Fred that he's still drinking and Mrs Bootle in the shop told you so, you know the price of lambs at the market and what old so-and-so down the road got from the organic butcher chappie, and I bet when Mrs Green comes in in a moment for her in-growing toenail you know the names and ages of each of her grandchildren.'

'She doesn't have grandchildren. Tom's not old enough, and Rebecca's still at university—'

'I rest my case,' he said drily, and Anna gave a self-conscious laugh.

'OK, I give up,' she said, a touch of mockery in her voice. 'Blame it on continuity. It might be something to do with the fact that I've been here off and on for the past thirty years. You might like to try it some time. Staying in one place has a lot to recommend it.'

She stripped off her gloves, bundled up all the disposable waste and put it in the yellow clinic waste bin.

Max watched her silently, making her antsy and nervous. 'Don't you have something useful to do, like look up Mrs Green's notes?' she asked acerbically.

One eyebrow arched expressively, but he turned to the paperwork on the desk and scanned it. 'She's on beta blockers,' he said thoughtfully. 'People sometimes get pincer nails with them. I wonder if that's what is wrong with her, or if she's got ordinary ingrowing toe-nails. The notes aren't very specific.'

Anna changed the paper over the couch, laid another trolley and turned to him. 'Shall I fetch her?'

'If it's not too much trouble,' he said mildly, and she pressed her lips together to hold back the retort and went out to find Mrs Green.

She limped across the waiting room, and Anna

frowned at her. 'You really are in a bad way, aren't you?' she said with sympathy.

'Oh, dear, don't talk about it! It's driving me mad. It's been getting worse and worse, but I've been ignoring it because Rebecca's home for the summer and I've been enjoying her company, but now I can't go anywhere with her and it's just ridiculous!'

'Don't worry, we'll soon have you sorted out. How's she getting on? Enjoying Liverpool?'

Mrs Green rolled her eyes. 'Oh, loves it! She says the social life is brilliant. Tom misses her, though. I didn't think he would because they fight all the time, but he's really enjoyed having her back for a while. I don't know what we'll do without her when she goes back.'

Mrs Green came to a halt just outside the door, and tugged at Anna's sleeve. 'This new man—Dr Carter. What's he like?' she whispered.

A total pain in the neck, she wanted to say, but professionalism prevailed. 'He's good,' she said truthfully. 'I'm sure you're in good hands.'

'Have you seen him do anything?'

She nodded. 'Yes—two ops this morning. He's very careful and thorough.'

Mrs Green relaxed visibly. 'Good,' she said in relief. 'I was so worried when I realised Suzanna had gone on maternity leave. I thought it wasn't for another week or so, but then I saw her in the shop yesterday and I was worried all night!'

Anna smiled and patted her arm. 'No need to worry. He's fine. Come on in, I'll introduce you. I'm sure you'll get on like a house on fire.'

Even if I don't, she added to herself. Except they had once, of course. They'd got on too well, from the moment they'd first clapped eyes on each other in the surgery in Gloucestershire...

'Hi.'

Anna looked up, straight into the most stunning blue eyes she'd ever seen, and felt her heart crash against her ribs.

'Hi,' she replied, and wondered if it was just her imagination or if she really sounded that breathless. 'Can I help you?'

'Tantalising thought,' he murmured, a lazy, sexy smile teasing those sensuous lips. 'Actually, I'm looking for the senior partner. I'm Max Carter, the locum.'

She took his outstretched hand, and felt a jolt of electricity up her arm. 'Anna Young. I'm the practice nurse. Well, I am at the moment. I expect I'll be tealady in a minute. John's out on a call. Shall I put the kettle on and fill you in?'

He followed her into the tiny kitchen, his presence making the air so thick with tension that she could hardly breathe, and watched her as she made coffee for them both.

'So, what's it like here?' he asked as they sipped their drinks a moment later.

'Crazy,' she said with a laugh. 'Everyone's lovely. All you need is a sense of humour and you'll survive.'

He did more than survive. He fitted right in, and every time Anna emerged from her room he seemed to be there. On his third day, he invited her out for a drink. She went, and it was wonderful. They shared the same zany sense of fun, liked the same music, chose the same food from the bar snacks menu.

Later that week he asked her out for dinner, and took her to an intimate, bijou little restaurant in Cheltenham where they ate lobster and crêpes and drank too much wine and laughed until the tears ran down their cheeks.

Then they came out of the restaurant and Max hailed a taxi, and when they fell into it, giggling, he looked at her and said, 'Where to?'

Suddenly the laughter died, replaced by a blazing heat which had been simmering gently under the surface for the whole week. 'You could come back for coffee,' she offered.

He nodded, and she leant forwards and told the taxi driver her address. Five minutes later they were there, letting themselves into the once-elegant Georgian terraced house where she had a flat.

They didn't bother with the coffee. Instead, as the door closed behind them they went into each other's arms, and their mouths met in hungry, devouring kisses that left them both aching for more.

He stayed that night, and the night after, and the night after that. Then it was Monday, and he was on call, and he went—reluctantly—back to his own flat and stayed there for a couple of nights.

He was tired. They both were, hardly having slept for the previous nights, and in order to preserve their sanity and professional competence they agreed to stay in their own homes. In practice this meant one or other of them getting up and getting dressed in the middle of the night, and after a while they gave up again and resigned themselves to exhaustion, unless Max was on call.

Then he stayed alone at his flat, and Anna missed him the entire time. They'd become so close it seemed strange to sleep without him, and Anna couldn't imagine them ever living apart.

Then, during the third week, Max became a little

distant. He seemed tired, more so than usual, and she sometimes caught a preoccupied expression on his face.

'Are you all right?' she asked him on one occasion.

He nodded. 'Yes, I'm fine. Just thinking about something.'

'A patient?'

He nodded. 'Yes, a patient,' he agreed.

'You shouldn't bring your work home,' she scolded gently, cuddling up to him. 'Want to talk about it?'

He shook his head. 'No. It's OK, really.' He turned his head and looked down at her, snuggled against his shoulder. 'Want to go to bed?'

She smiled. 'I always want to go to bed with you,' she teased.

His smile was thin and weary. 'I could do with sleeping,' he warned. 'Don't expect a wild night of passion.'

She chuckled and stood up, pulling him to his feet. 'You can sleep. There's always the morning.'

But in the morning he was gone when she woke, and she found him at work, peering at something down the microscope they used for quick checks on bloods and things.

'You sneaked off,' she grumbled gently, standing behind him and hugging him over the back of the chair.

'Sorry. Work to do,' he told her, still peering.

She let him go and went into the kitchen, putting the kettle on. When she came back out he was putting some samples into a path lab envelope. 'I just want to take these up to the lab,' he said, and left her there.

She shrugged, made herself some tea and curled up in the corner, scanning through her notes for the morning surgery and mentally checking that she had the inoculations she was going to need. It was OK.

Everything was fine, and she settled back and finished her tea and wondered what specimens he'd taken to the lab.

Odd, at that time of the day. Oh, well. Perhaps it was some histological sample he'd taken the day before. Maybe he was in a hurry for the result.

They went out for dinner again that night, and afterwards they went back to her flat.

He wasn't tired that night, she thought. Far from it. Their lovemaking reached new heights, and left them both shaken with the intensity of it.

'I love you,' she said softly, and his arms tightened convulsively.

'Anna,' he whispered.

He didn't say the little words, but she knew he meant them.

At least, she thought she did.

Then she woke in the morning to find him gone, a note from him propped up against the kettle. It filled her with foreboding, and she held it with trembling fingers for an age before she could open it.

Dear Anna,

By the time you see this I'll be gone. I'm sorry to leave you like this, but I can't stay. There are all sorts of reasons why I have to go, but I'll miss you, you've been a lot of fun. Don't have regrets. Life's too short for regrets. Just remember the good times.

Max

Not even 'love, Max'. Just 'Max'.

She screwed up the note and threw it in the bin, then, without even stopping to dress, she jumped in her car and drove to his flat. He was gone, a neighbour told her, peering curiously at her nightdress.

She went home, curled up in a chair and howled. Handfuls of soggy tissue later, she had a bath, got dressed and walked miles, ranting at him as she paced up and down the Cotswold hills in a fury of bitter recriminations and desperate longing.

He couldn't have gone—not for ever! How would she cope without him?

She phoned her mother and blurted out the whole sorry mess, and her mother gave her telephone hugs and said, 'Come home for the weekend.' So she did.

And there, lo and behold, was a vacancy for a practice nurse. Too gutted to stay in Cheltenham, she handed in her notice, moved back to Wenham Market and then discovered to her absolute horror that she was expecting a baby.

Anna deliberated for ages, then wrote a letter to Max and waited with bated breath for his reply.

It never came. All that came was her own letter, with RETURN TO SENDER-NOT KNOWN AT THIS ADDRESS stamped all over it.

She tried again, but the same thing happened.

She wrote to the locum agency that he'd come through, asking for a new forwarding address, but was told that he'd stopped working for them and there was no way to contact him.

So that was that. She had a baby on the way, no father on the horizon, a job she was about to have to give up. Without the love and support of her parents and the practice staff, she would have sunk without trace.

Then Harry was born, undoubtedly the best thing that had ever happened to her in the whole of her twenty-six years, and she put thoughts of Max on the side and concentrated on giving her baby the best start in life she could manage.

It was hard—impossibly hard at first—and financially always difficult, but she managed, and it had slowly grown easier. People had accepted her and Harry, and she'd felt very much a part of the community.

And it had been fine until last week, when Max had turned up again out of the blue and thrown her carefully ordered emotions into pandemonium.

He finished Mrs Green's foot, leaving her with just the central section of the nail so that the painful tightly curled edges were gone and wouldn't trouble her again. Anna bandaged the battered and bloody toe and reflected that she hadn't registered anything he had done.

She'd been miles away, reliving those wonderfully romantic moments in his arms, and it seemed almost intrusive of him and Mrs Green to be there. She'd tuned them out so absolutely that she wondered if she'd done anything stupid.

Apparently not, because Max said nothing, and he would have done. He didn't tend to hold back.

The rest of the day was routine and passed without incident, until she reached the end of her day. Then she found a note from Max in Reception.

Would like to come round tonight to see photos etc. Would nine o'clock be all right? That should give you time to put Harry to bed. Leave me a note to confirm.

M

Not even 'Max'. He was getting briefer, she thought drily. Soon he'd be signing things with a cross.

'Nine is fine. See you later. Anna.' Her reply was even more brief.

She went home, looked around and had a guilt-driven tidying fit. Then she shoved the vacuum round, rescued Harry's toys from the dust collector and wormed the cat, which took the hump and stalked off, tail twitching furiously.

'Bedtime,' she said to Harry at seven-thirty.

He whinged, grumbled and squirmed all the way up the stairs, through the bath and into bed, but in the end he fell asleep in seconds.

Then, just when she thought she might grab a moment to change and clean herself up, the doorbell rang.

She opened the door to find Max there, looking disgustingly appealing in a faded blue shirt, which matched the changing blue of his eyes, and a pair of jeans that did wicked and wholly unprintable things to his body.

Help, she thought, I'm going to be alone with him!

She took him into the sitting room, put on the overhead light on maximum and pulled out the baby albums, then headed for a chair. 'Here you go. Baby photos.'

He sat down next to her and took the albums, then lifted the first one. He opened the cover, stared at the pictures for a moment then closed his eyes.

'I'm sorry you had to go through it alone,' he said heavily.

'You could have been there, if you hadn't disappeared so effectively. I tried to write, but there was no getting through to you. Not known at this address and all that. Anyway, Mum was with me.'

He nodded, then looked down at the pictures again. She glanced across, and felt her face colour. He was looking at a picture of her breast-feeding the newborn Harry.

'I'd forgotten that one was in there,' she muttered, embarrassed that he should see something so personal.

'It's beautiful,' he said softly. 'I'm glad you breast-fed him. There's something so primitive—so erotic and right about it. I wish I could have seen it.'

'You could have seen it. All you had to do was stick around,' she reminded him—again.

He shook his head. 'No.' He turned the pages in silence, except for the odd question, and she could feel the tension radiating off him.

After a while he shut the albums and stood up. 'I think I'll call it a night, I'm tired. Mind if we do this again? I'd like to ask you more.'

She realised with a shock that it was after eleven o'clock.

'Sure. Not tomorrow, I've got something on. Maybe Thursday?'

His mouth moved automatically in a polite, social smile. 'That would be lovely,' he agreed, and turned away, but not before she'd seen the pain in his eyes.

He could have been there—he could have had it all, she reminded herself as she watched him walk away. He could have, and he'd chosen not to.

Well, having made the bed, he could lie in it, she thought crossly, and tried not to remember the pain in his eyes or the weary set of his shoulders.

It was five years too late to appeal to her sense of decency. Frankly, he was lucky she was prepared to do this much.

She closed the door, turned off the sitting-room light

and went to bed, evicting the cat from the middle of it. He came back, though, and she let him. He was undemanding company, and conversation with him wasn't complicated by lies and half-truths and mixed emotions.

It took her ages to go to sleep.

CHAPTER THREE

'IS THERE any chance you could get a babysitter for tomorrow?' Max asked Anna the following morning.

She stared at him, puzzled and a little suspicious. 'A babysitter? I thought you were coming to me. That's what we agreed.'

He looked down at his hand, his fingers tracing a pattern on the edge of the desk. 'I thought perhaps you could come to me—I could cook something.'

She laughed. 'You? Cook? No,' she said bluntly. It was too scary—too much like a date, and that made her nervous. She had weak enough defences around him, without him setting up some big seduction scene.

He sighed. 'I'm not trying to proposition you, Annie,' he said, proving for the nth time that he could read her mind. 'I just want to be able to talk openly, and with Harry in the house it's difficult. Anyway, there's something I want to tell you.'

'So tell me,' she said bluntly. 'Whatever it is, just tell me. It can't be that secret or important.'

His face closed, and she thought she'd been a little harsh, but he needed to know that he didn't affect her any longer. She *had* to have some distance, or she was going to go crazy.

'Forget it,' he said, a little shortly. 'You're probably right. It isn't that important.' He scooped up a pile of notes, turned on his heel and headed for the door, leaving her in the office with a terrible suspicion that she had just made a very hurtful mistake.

'So what? He hurt you,' she muttered under her breath.

David Fellows came up behind her and put an arm around her shoulders. 'All right, my dear?' he asked, an expression of concern on his face.

She shrugged and eased out of reach. 'Fine. Busy.' And I'm not going to discuss Max with you, she thought, however kindly you might be.

'Just wondered. You've been looking a bit preoccupied recently. Nothing to do with Max, is it?'

'Of course not. We're just colleagues,' she said firmly, and headed for her room and a bit of peace and privacy.

Her patients provided a little light relief that morning—children for inoculation, an elderly lady for an ulcer dressing, Mr Bryant with his sinus on his finger for a fresh dressing on the incision—she knew them all, and chatted happily to them, pushing Max Carter to the back of her mind.

He didn't stay there, though. She worried about whatever it was he'd wanted to tell her, and her callous dismissal of its importance, and after lunch she sought him out in the little garden behind the practice and apologised.

'You got me too early in the morning—never was a morning person, remember?' she added with a wry smile, and then regretted it, because all sorts of warm and intimate images came flooding back to her and swamped her reason.

'Yes, I remember,' he said softly, and she knew that he was remembering, too. Oh, darn. Why had she brought it up?

'Anyway,' she went on, 'if you still want me to come over—yes, I could get a babysitter. I think you're right, it would be easier to talk about Harry if he wasn't in the house. He comes downstairs sometimes to find me, and I wouldn't want him to overhear something that upset or confused him.'

Max nodded agreement. 'That was what I thought. If it's the idea of my cooking that's putting you off, don't worry,' he said, a slow, teasing smile playing around his lips. 'I've learned to be quite self-sufficient in the past few years.'

'Just something simple,' she warned him. 'No candlelight or rubbish like that, or I go straight back home again.'

He smiled. 'No candlelight. There's a fluorescent strip light in the kitchen-breakfast room of my cottage—will that do you?'

'Perfect,' she said crisply. 'What time? I need to arrange the babysitter.'

'Eight? Eight-thirty? What time does Harry go to bed?'

'Six-thirty. He gets up with the lark, disgustingly cheerful,' she told him flatly. 'It's another fault inherited from his father.'

Max grinned. 'Is that right? It must be hell for you.'

'Trust me, it is. Right, I must ring the sitter and get back to work. I've got another surgery starting in a minute.'

She went back inside, leaving him sitting there on the edge of a low wall in the sunshine, surrounded by all the greenery of the garden. She glanced back, and found his eyes on her, regarding her thoughtfully. For a moment their eyes locked, and then his mouth twitched in a travesty of a smile. She turned away, suddenly hot, and wondered if she'd actually survive the evening with him without sacrificing her principles and falling into bed.

More to the point, did she *want* to survive in this emotional and physical vacuum she'd been in for so many years? She thought again of their lazy mornings, the gentle, teasing, sensual way he'd woken her, and she almost moaned aloud.

He had been so tender, so clever, so incredibly good at making her feel well loved. He'd been so good at it that she'd never had the desire or inclination to try again with anyone else. It hadn't seemed fair to the very few kind, pleasant men with whom she'd had low-key, short-term relationships to expose them to certain failure.

She pushed the thought from her mind and rang her neighbour, Jill Fraser, arranging for her to have Harry for the night. They worked a reciprocal system, and it saved her having to overuse her parents and wear out their goodwill—and just at the moment Jill owed her loads of time. Anna had had her three children more times than she cared to remember just recently, since Jill's husband had walked out yet again.

She'd been able to sympathise. At least Harry's father had only left her with one child, and he'd had the grace to disappear and stay away—until now. No, she thought, she didn't want to rekindle the flames of her old romance. It would be emotional suicide. She'd just deal with the business of Harry's photos and so on, and hear what he had to say.

She wondered yet again what it was Max wanted to tell her. Was he married?

The thought chilled her. 'You're stupid,' she growled at herself. 'You don't want him anyway—how can it make any difference if he's married? He's probably going to tell you he's only here for a week.'

She resigned herself to waiting for their meeting on Thursday night, and concentrated on her patients. It was a short day for a change, with no evening surgery for her, and she picked up Harry from her mother and took him for a walk, then did some washing, tidied up and threw the cat's bed in the washing machine, to his utter disgust.

He decamped to her best tapestry cushion, and sat there, sulking, for the rest of the night, before joining her on her bed.

'You are a nuisance,' she told him firmly, shoving him out of the way, but he purred and rubbed himself against her face, leaving hairs stuck all over it.

'Oh, cat,' she grumbled, wiping the hairs away and pushing him down the bed again to the bottom. 'You could go outside and hunt mice, if you were a respectable cat instead of a fat and indolent pyjama case.'

'Mreouw,' he squawked, and settled down with a sigh to lick himself thoroughly from end to end.

'You'll get hairballs,' she said self-righteously, tugging the pillow into the side of her neck and wondering what Max had to say.

A chilling thought occurred to her. What if he'd never married or had children because he had an inheritable disorder? Some recessive gene he carried, or some bizarre and insidious disease that only showed itself in later life? Maybe he wanted to warn her that Harry would inherit it?

Panic washed over her, and she got out of bed and made herself a hot drink, pacing round the house as she drank it.

'You're mad,' she told herself at three in the morning, when she was on her third hot chocolate. 'It's nothing. It will be about something totally inconsequential, and you'll laugh at yourself. He said it wasn't important. Just wait. You'll find out soon enough.'

She went back to bed, evicted the cat from the warm, snuggly bit between the top of the quilt and the pillow, and lay down in a sea of hair.

Darned cat. She turned the pillow over, shifted the quilt and eventually fell asleep. Two hours later Harry climbed into bed with her and woke her by the simple expedient of peeling back her eyelids and saying hello.

She groaned and reached for him, pulling him under the quilt and snuggling him for a moment. Sometimes he'd go back to sleep again but, just her luck, this time he refused. Bouncingly, revoltingly cheerful, he sat up and pulled the quilt off her and grinned.

'Breakfast time,' he announced, and dragged her down the stairs to the kitchen.

'Harry, it's only six-thirty,' she wailed, trailing after him. 'We don't have to get up till seven-thirty.'

'But I'm hungry,' he said reasonably, squirming into the cereal cupboard and coming out with his favourite box. He handed it to her expectantly and, resigned, she switched on the kettle, poured his cereal out into his bowl, sloshed milk onto it and flopped into a chair.

The cat appeared, meowing and trying to look cute, and she sighed and fed him as well.

'Where yours?' Harry asked through a mouthful of cereal.

'I'm not hungry,' she told him, getting up to make her tea. Six or seven cups should do it, she thought with slight hysteria, and pulled down a mug from the cupboard.

It said WORLD'S BEST MUM on the outside, and

she loved it. She filled it with steaming tea, splashed a bit of milk in and hoofed the cat off her chair, before slumping into it and listening, eyes closed, to the sound of Harry chomping.

Max was puzzled. He had a patient, a woman of fifty called Valerie Hawkshead, who was complaining of headaches and light-headedness. She had slight arthritis, muscular aches and pains but was otherwise healthy. According to the notes, she took pills for the aches and pains, and they used to work for the headaches, but they didn't seem so effective any longer and she was starting to forget things and wondered if she was getting Alzheimer's.

Suzanna had made a note that she thought the headaches were from analgesic over-use, and she'd eased her off them and put her on an anti-anxiety drug and done a battery of tests, all normal.

Now today she was back with her husband, looking slightly unkempt and withdrawn, and according to her husband she'd lost weight.

Max tried a mini-mental state test, and she scored 12 out of 30—hardly bothering to respond to some of the questions. That didn't seem to him like the reaction of a woman suffering from analgesic over-use, or even marked anxiety. It was something more than that, his intuition told him—something deeper.

More sinister.

Max trusted his intuition.

'I want to refer you to a neurologist,' he said. 'He can examine you and see if he can get to the bottom of the headaches and forgetfulness. OK?'

They were quite happy, and so he sent them off and dictated the letter later. Hopefully the neurologist would pick up on any problem. In the meantime, he had Annie coming round that evening for a meal. The place looked even drabber than usual and he still had to go shopping for some of the ingredients.

Just so long as Mrs Bootle had red and green peppers, courgettes and mushrooms he'd be all right. Knowing his luck, though, they'd come on Friday for the weekend, which wouldn't help him tonight.

He checked his watch, debated whether or not he'd got time and rang the shop. 'I don't suppose you could put a few things together for me, could you?' he asked Mrs Bootle, and she agreed without hesitation.

He dictated his list, gave up on the durum wheat flour and ploughed on with his surgery until he'd finished it. Then he glanced at his watch.

Six-thirty, and he hadn't even picked up the shopping or started the main dish. By seven he was home, by seven-thirty he was on his way to the shower, with the sauce bubbling on the back of the stove and the pasta piled up ready, and before he was finished and organised, the doorbell rang.

'You're being silly,' Anna told herself twelve hours after her revoltingly early breakfast. She had a whole plethora of outfits spread around her bedroom, and not one of them did she deem suitable.

Jeans were too casual, the trouser suit was too formal, the dress was too eveningy, the skirt was boring and she wore it for going to the dentist and things like that.

Which left the long, soft cotton dress that clung and draped and was both casual and dressy, and which she felt good in. Max had never seen it before, but that wasn't a problem with the majority of her wardrobe. So far he'd only seen her uniform and her jeans.

She turned her attention to her hair. Up or down? She chewed her lip, brushing out the long strands and studying it critically.

Down. No, up.

She threw the brush across the room, went into the bathroom and showered with undue care and scented shower gel, all the while getting more and more irritated with herself because it wasn't supposed to be like this and it shouldn't matter what she wore or how she smelt or if her hair was up, down or dropping out!

His cottage was on the outskirts of town, down a secluded little lane. It was in a lovely setting but it was looking a little tired. For the umpteenth time she wondered why he didn't settle down and buy himself a nice house, even if he didn't want to get married and have children and ties. She rang the doorbell and waited, and heard his footsteps running down stairs.

He opened the door, wearing only a pair of jeans and a T-shirt, bare feet sticking out from the bottom of the jeans. He looked gorgeous, and all the reasons why this was a bad idea came crashing back to her.

He grinned, making it even worse. 'Sorry, I'm on the drag. I was cooking and got carried away and forgot the time. Come on in.' He led her through to the kitchen, giving her a tempting view of firm, hard thighs and a neat bottom snugly encased in worn, soft denim the exact shade of his incredibly lovely eyes.

She sighed quietly. How could he have so much power over her still? He'd walked out on her, leaving just a short, unemotional note that trampled her dreams in the dust, and yet still she only had to look at him and her knees went weak.

Hormones, she told herself. There had been something in the news about falling in love being like a psychiatric illness, altering levels of certain hormones in the body and changing behaviour. At the time she'd recognised the syndrome as something from which she'd thought she'd recovered.

Now, following him through the little cottage, she wasn't so sure.

They went into the kitchen so he could check on the pasta sauce that was bubbling gently on the hob, and he offered her a glass of wine.

Trying to soften her up to seduce her? He didn't need any help. 'I'll have water, please,' she said, and he pulled a bottle of mineral water from the fridge.

'This all right?'

She nodded, surprised that he would have anything so—what? Civilised? He used to poke fun at people who paid huge sums of money for bottled water, and here he was with his own supply!

That wasn't the only change, she realised as they ate. He could cook now, too, probably better than she could.

'This is delicious,' she told him appreciatively, twirling strands of pasta round her fork. 'Where did you learn to make such a lovely sauce—or did you cheat and buy it?'

He chuckled. 'In Italy,' he told her, leaning back in his chair and sipping his wine thoughtfully. 'I spent six months there, doing a little locum job. It was fun. I lived with a real Italian mama, and she took me under her wing. I learned to cook all sorts of things. I made the pasta, too. It's a handy little skill—it's dead easy and it impresses people no end.'

It worked—she was impressed. She was also falling

under his spell again, and to keep her emotional distance was getting harder and harder.

She had to keep reminding herself that leopards didn't change their spots, and if he'd walked out on her once, he could do it again, but her warnings fell on deaf ears.

She succumbed to a glass of wine, then another, and they settled down on the sofa with the pictures of Harry, and she told him all about her pregnancy and his birth, and how kind everyone had been.

'I missed you, though,' she told him, not meaning to but finding the words just spilling out. 'Even though you'd walked out like that, I still missed you.'

He bowed his head. 'I'm sorry,' he murmured. 'It was hell for you, and I should have been there.'

Was it genuine remorse in his voice? It sounded like it. 'I tried to tell you about it,' she said, 'but my letters came back. You'd moved, or just returned them. I don't know.'

'I moved.'

She nodded. 'I hadn't—but I suppose you didn't want to know anyway, or you would have kept in touch.'

His hand came up and cupped her cheek. 'I'm sorry,' he said gruffly. Their eyes locked, and after the longest moment, as if in slow motion, his head descended.

She had plenty of time to move, to get away from him, to do what she'd said she'd do and stop anything like this happening. Instead, like a traitor, her arm stole round his neck and drew him down, and their lips met.

It was like coming home.

After all these years, she could still remember the feel of his mouth, the texture of his skin, the firm pressure of his lips. He tasted of coffee and mints and a lingering trace of brandy, and she moaned softly and threaded her fingers through his hair, urging him closer.

He shifted against her, drawing her body up against his and deepening the kiss. She felt the velvet sweep of his tongue, the gentle coaxing pressure of his lips, and she forgot all her warnings to herself.

This was where she belonged—here, with him, in this embrace. His hand left her cheek and trailed softly, tormentingly down, to settle lightly on her breast. She arched against it and he squeezed gently, making her ache with longing.

'Max,' she sighed against his lips, and his breath drifted raggedly over her cheek.

'Let me love you,' he whispered unevenly, and the longing grew until she nearly cried out.

'Yes,' she whimpered, 'oh, yes. Please.'

He stood up and drew her to her feet, leading her upstairs to the bedroom. She didn't notice it—didn't notice anything except the feel of his arm around her shoulders, the hard jut of his hipbone against her side, the heat of his body radiating through his clothes.

He stripped them off, then with shaking hands he took the hem of her dress and peeled it gently over her head.

She felt suddenly naked and vulnerable, standing there in her basic chainstore bra and pants. Would he notice the changes in her body? The thickening of her waist, the little bulge below her tummy button where her muscles hadn't quite gone flat after Harry?

Her breasts weren't as firm, either—would he mind? Would it put him off?

'You're lovely,' he said unsteadily. 'Oh, Annie, I've missed you so much…'

He held his arms out to her, and she flew into them,

clinging to him and letting herself absorb the feel of his body. She was right, he was thinner. Leaner, really, perhaps more mature—and hot. So hot. She ran her hands down the firm column of his spine, and he moved against her restlessly.

'I need you,' he whispered, his breath teasing at her hair, and she took his hand and led him to the bed, sinking down onto it and drawing him down beside her.

He was shaking all over, his body trembling under her hands, and he couldn't unfasten her bra. She slipped the catch and threw it aside, and his hands were there to catch her and cradle the soft warmth of her breasts.

His mouth was hot, closing over one aching, straining peak, his palm roughly caressing the other while she cried out with need. 'You're so lovely,' he said, his lips trailing down over her hipbone and laying soft, hot kisses against the curve of her thigh.

'Max, please…!'

He stripped away their last remaining scraps of clothing, then moved over her, his body meshing with hers in one smooth, effortless homecoming that made her cry out with joy.

'Oh, Max,' she sobbed, and he trapped her face between his hands and plundered her mouth. She moved restlessly against him, and with a ragged groan he gave up all pretence of control and drove into her, sending her over the brink into glorious freefall.

She heard his cry, felt the stiffening of his body against hers, and then they were drifting slowly back down to earth, cradled in each other's arms. Tears clogged her lashes and threatened to choke her, and she turned her head into his neck and bit her lip. She wouldn't cry. She wouldn't…

'Oh, Annie, I've missed you,' he said, and his voice cracked. His head dropped against her shoulder, his chest heaved and she gave up her feeble attempt at controlling her own tears and let them fall.

Five years, she thought. I've longed for him for five years. He's my other half, the other part of me, and he's come back. All the anger, all the bitterness—just a defence, because I love him, and I always have, and I always will.

He lifted his head and kissed away her tears, his own eyes deep pools of emotion. 'It's been so long,' he murmured. 'I thought I must have exaggerated what it was like for us—thought my memory must have built it up into something that it wasn't—but I was wrong. It was every bit as beautiful as I remember—maybe even better.'

She thought he was going to say more—perhaps tell her that he loved her—but he turned his head away, dragging in a deep breath and letting it out on a shaky sigh.

He rolled away from her, collapsing onto the bed beside her, and drew her up against his side, his hand idly smoothing the skin of her back with slow, lazy strokes.

So where do we go from here? she wondered as she lay cradled in the crook of his arm, her legs tangled with his and her ear listening to the steady rhythm of his heart. Did she dare to hope this time? He was older now, more mature. Would he stay? Or would he go again, leaving her in tatters once more?

'I don't have ties,' he'd said.

Perhaps Harry would have the power to change him, where she had failed. It was unlikely, and a few days ago she would have said impossible. The other night it had sounded as if he didn't want anything to do with the boy apart from a periodical update. Now he made it sound as if she were the most wonderful woman he'd ever met, and he'd missed her.

Would it be enough, this time?

'I need a drink—shall I bring a bottle of water back to bed?' he murmured, hugging her gently against his side.

'Please.'

He slid out of the bed, padding soundlessly across the room and down the stairs. She heard him pottering about, and sat up, naked, on the bed, her arms hugging her knees. While she waited for him to come back, she looked around her at the little bedroom of his rented home.

It was lit only by the soft glow coming from the bedside lamp he'd turned on when they'd entered the room, and even in the mellow light it was bleak, lacking warmth and character, and she felt sad for him that he seemed to live permanently in these sorts of surroundings. It just seemed so—temporary, really. Rootless. As if it didn't matter.

The night had grown cool, and the slight breeze from the open window dallied over her skin, pebbling her nipples and bringing goose-bumps up all over her. She gave a little shiver, and stood up, pulling the quilt back. It was silly to be cold.

She was about to climb back in under the covers when she spotted a piece of paper on the floor by the bed, sent flying, no doubt, by their hasty disrobing. She picked it up, glancing at it out of idle curiosity, and felt the blood drain from her face.

It was a letter to Max, telling him when his next appointment had been scheduled for.

Nothing odd in that, except that it was from the hospital that housed the country's foremost oncology unit.

And Max had an appointment there, which could only mean one thing...

Anna closed her eyes, then opened them again and re-read the letter in case she'd made a mistake.

No. There it was in black and white, directed to him at a London address, presumably his last temporary post.

And, suddenly, it all fell into place. The constant moving around, the refusal to settle or have ties, the lack of commitment to anywhere or anything—all typical of a man under a death sentence.

How long had it been going on? A year? Two?

Horror trickled over her like cold water.

Now that she'd found him again, was she about to lose him?

'Here—I've brought us some goodies to snack on.'

She turned her head slowly and looked up at him, the letter lying unnoticed in her nerveless fingers.

'What does this mean?' she asked him with deadly calm, fluttering the sheet of paper.

He glanced down, and sighed. 'Oh, hell,' he said softly.

'Hell what? What does it mean? Max, tell me what's wrong with you,' she said, mustering as much firmness as she could.

He put the tray down on the bedside table, took the letter from her and put it down as well, then wrapped her hands in his.

'It's a follow-up appointment,' he said softly.

'I can see that,' she said, dreading his answer but

needing to hear it—needing to have her fears confirmed. 'What for? Why?'

He took a long breath, then met her searching eyes. 'That's what I was going to tell you. I've got non-Hodgkin's lymphoma.'

CHAPTER FOUR

SHOCK held Anna motionless for an endless moment, then she snatched her hands free and stood up, crossing to the window and wrapping her arms around her waist.

Lymphoma.

Oh, God, no.

It was dark outside, only the distant lights of the village breaking the velvet blackness. She shivered in the cool stream of air, and then felt a soft towelling robe settle comfortingly around her shoulders. Max's hands cupped her arms, drawing her back against him.

'I told you it wasn't important,' she said in a hollow, incredulous voice. 'I had no idea—'

'Of course you didn't. It doesn't matter.'

'It does!' she cried softly, turning in his arms and looking up into those beautiful blue eyes. They were in shadow and she couldn't read them, but his hand came up and cupped her cheek, and his thumb caressed her jaw with tender, slow strokes.

'I'm glad we made love before you found out. Otherwise I might have thought it was pity. You know—last privileges for a condemned man and all that.' He smiled, a wry, crooked smile that tore at her heart.

Tears swam in her eyes, but she blinked them away. 'Don't,' she protested. Her arms slid round him, and she buried her face in his chest and bit her lip hard. 'How long?' she mumbled.

'How long have I had it? Five years.'

Her head came up sharply. 'Five years? So you knew? When you were with me, you knew?'

'I began to suspect. I'd found a lump in my groin— just a pea, really, nothing significant. It didn't hurt, I had no other symptoms. I thought it was just a lymphatic reaction to infection, probably—something I didn't know I'd done. A little cut, a splinter or something. I couldn't find anything, and it didn't go away.'

'So what did you do?'

'I took a biopsy and sent it off.'

'Yourself?'

He nodded. 'And it came back positive. I went to an oncologist privately and he confirmed low-grade follicular non-Hodgkin's lymphoma. That was the day before I left.'

She eased away from him, sliding her arms into the sleeves of his dressing-gown and belting it tightly, as if to protect her from what she was hearing.

'Why did you leave?' she asked desperately. 'Why like that, with just that note? Why didn't you tell me?' Her voice was starting to crack, and she wheeled away, going to stand by the window and staring out into the dark, quiet night. In the distance a dog barked. She hardly registered it. All she could think was that he'd gone, run away when he should have stayed and talked it through with her. If he'd loved her at all—

'I wanted to protect you. We hardly knew each other, Annie. It wasn't fair to expect you to go through all that with me.'

'All what?' she stormed, turning on him furiously. 'Sharing the burden? Supporting you in your treatment? Cheering you up and helping you when you were down?'

'Exactly,' he said sadly. 'How could I ask that of

you after only three weeks—even if they were the best and most wonderful three weeks of my life? I missed you, Annie. Believe me, it was the hardest thing I've ever done, and so many times I nearly tried to contact you.'

'You should have done.'

He shook his head. 'Why? To tell you I wasn't in remission any more? That it had come back, and was threatening me again? Or the next time? Or when I was lying in hospital, being blasted by drugs before having the stem cell treatment as a last-ditch attempt at knocking·it on the head?'

He laughed softly. 'You wouldn't have wanted me, Annie. I was thin to the point of gaunt, I looked like death. I'd lost my hair, I'd lost my faith in myself. I wasn't worth having.'

Tears welled up and scalded her cheeks. 'Oh, Max. Do you really think that would have made any difference to me? I would have been there for you.'

'Sacrificing yourself. I thought if I left you, you might find someone else—someone you could marry and have children with. It was the only thing that comforted me, thinking that you might have found happiness.'

She laughed, a tiny, humourless huff of sound. 'Happiness? Yes, I found happiness, eventually. With your son. *Our* son.' She clenched her fists, hanging onto her temper by a hair. 'You had no *right* to make that decision for me. It was my decision to make, not yours.'

He was silent for a while, then shook his head. 'Maybe I didn't want you there,' he said softly.

She felt the rejection right through to her bones. It held her stunned, unable to move, to breathe, to think.

She dragged in a lungful of air and let it out again

in a whoosh. 'I'll go,' she whispered, frantically scrabbling around on the floor for her clothes. 'If you don't want me here...'

'Annie, stop it.'

'I can't stop it,' she wept. 'Just let me go.'

'No.' His hands came out and caught her shoulders, drawing her up against his chest. 'No, Annie, don't run. Stay and talk about it—'

'No!' She drummed her fists against his chest impotently. 'Max, please!'

'Shh.' His hands soothed her, stroking slowly up and down her spine, and she sagged against him, sobbing helplessly.

'It's all right, my love,' he murmured, but she knew he was lying. It wasn't all right, and it hadn't been all right in a long, long time, and it probably never would be again.

What if he'd died? She would never have known! All these years she'd pictured him with another woman, and instead he'd been ill, fighting death alone...

'You should have told me!' she yelled, pummelling his chest again, the hot tears refusing to be held in check.

'I'm sorry. Maybe I should have done. I just wanted to spare you the pain. It was such a brief affair. I thought you'd get over me.'

She dropped her hands and moved away, drawing herself up and hugging her arms around her waist again to distance herself. 'Well, I didn't. I still love you. So what happens now?'

He sighed. 'I don't know. I'm in remission at the moment. It's as near as I'll get to a cure. It may come back, it may not. They may be able to destroy it again if it comes back, they may not. I have no idea. It's just one of those damn things, like dog muck on your shoe. You can wipe it off, you can get rid of it, but that last trace seems to linger.'

He shrugged. 'You just learn to live with it. It's like asthma or high blood pressure or diabetes. You treat it, you deal with it, and you know that it will probably kill you in the end, but it's a vague sort of end. It may be years—many, many years. A lifetime. It may be just a few short months. No one knows. That's the hardest thing to deal with, to learn to live with—the terrible uncertainty. It's like the sword of Damocles hanging over you, held by a bit of frayed thread. I couldn't ask you to share that, and I wouldn't.'

She swallowed, trying to visualise such an uncertain future. No wonder he wouldn't settle down.

'What about Harry?' she asked, choked by tears. 'Is he ever going to know you're his father?'

'No.'

'But he has a right—'

'He has a right to a secure future. He has a right to happiness, and confidence in his own mortality. I won't take that away from him, Anna, and I won't let you do it either.'

Anna. He'd called her Anna.

It made her feel cold inside.

'He has a right to his father, too.'

'To watch me die? To watch me endure another series of treatments? To not know if this time I'm coming home?'

'Yes! Yes, he has that right. He's a human—he's not just a child. You can't shield him from reality. People get ill. That's why I'm a nurse and you're a doctor. And people die.'

But not you. Please, God, not you. She turned away, blinking hard and biting her lip until she could taste the salt of her blood.

'Annie.' His voice was soft, his hands gentle. 'Come to bed. Let me hold you.'

She turned, burrowing into his chest, and he led her to the bed and tucked her under the quilt, their snack forgotten. He held her close, his heartbeat steady under her ear, and he seemed so alive, so well and normal and vital that she could hardly believe what he'd told her.

Maybe she'd wake up soon and find it was all a dream?

Max held her, his hands moving rhythmically over her shoulders and down her back, soothing her. Tears clogged his lashes, and he blinked them away. They could have had so much together.

He tipped her chin, his mouth finding hers and kissing her tenderly, and she clung to him, kissing him back as if she was starving for him.

Maybe she was. He understood that.

He peeled away the dressing-gown and kissed every inch of her, noting the changes—the softer fullness of her breasts, the gentle curve of her abdomen, the slight widening of her hips. She'd lost that youthfulness, become a ripe, fertile woman in her prime, and he found her somehow more beautiful, more intoxicating than the slender girl she'd been.

Her hands were all over him, fluttering feverishly as he teased and tormented her with hot, suckling kisses and sliding caresses. 'Please,' she begged, and he moved over her, his body trembling with the effort of holding back his own response.

She felt so good. So well. So alive. He sought her

mouth frantically, as if he could draw life from her to conquer the demon that stalked him.

He felt her body start to tighten, and she bucked beneath him, crying out. He caught her cries, their kiss muffling his deep groan as his body stiffened against her, shuddering with the force of his release.

'I love you,' she whispered, and he couldn't hold the tears any longer. They fell on her face, running down into her hair, mingling with her own as they welled from her beautiful eyes.

'I'm sorry,' he said raggedly. 'Annie, I'm sorry.' He didn't know what he was sorry for—for dragging her into this sorry mess, for leaving her the first time, or because he was going to leave her again.

And this time, he'd make sure it was for ever...

'You can't go,' she said flatly. 'You have to stop running. You have a son. Even if I don't mean anything to you, he should. At least get to know him, even if you don't tell him who you are. You can at least spend some time with him, with us. I can tell him you're here for a while and you're lonely, and so we're going to be your friends.'

'And then leave, when Suzanna comes back to work? Walk out on you again?'

She shook her head, trying to stay calm. 'I would like you to stay—or take us with you.'

'I can't. I won't.'

'You don't know that. Give yourself time. Max, I'm a health professional. I understand that we can't save everyone. What I do, as a nurse, is improve quality of life. There are many ways of doing that and, if you've only got a limited amount of time, don't you owe it to yourself to make that time happy?'

His jaw clenched, and he turned away. 'I can't, Anna,' he said in a strangled voice. 'Don't push me, please.'

'At least stay until Suzanna comes back,' she pleaded. 'Even if you don't see Harry, at least stay with me. Let me have some memories—please?'

He looked back at her, his eyes tortured. 'You don't know what you're asking,' he said roughly.

'Yes, I do. I know exactly what I'm asking, and I know it takes courage—more courage than running away again.'

She let the words hang, and after a while he bowed his head and gave a heavy sigh. 'I'll think about it.'

Her shoulders dropped with relief. It was only a slight concession, but at least she wasn't going to come out of her morning surgery and find him gone.

'Just promise me something—if you decide you have to go, say goodbye. Don't leave me again—not like that.'

He nodded slowly. 'All right.'

'Thank you.'

She wheeled round and yanked his consulting-room door open, almost running down the corridor to her room. She had five minutes before her first patient— five minutes to get her wildly see-sawing emotions under control and dredge up a professional demeanour.

She managed it, but only just.

Mr Bryant came in to see her for his dressing, and looked at her keenly. He'd known her all her life, and she just hoped he wouldn't say anything kind, or she'd dissolve.

'You look a bit wat'ry, my dear,' he said as she bent over his finger. 'Took the hay fever, have you?'

She nodded, hoping he wouldn't know she'd never

suffered so much as a single sneeze from a pollen allergy. 'It must be bad at the moment—there must be something about that gets to me.'

Called Max, she added to herself, and dismissed the thought firmly. She had to work, had to concentrate and deal with her patients. It would give it time to sink in, give her subconscious time to assimilate it.

'It's looking better,' she told Mr Bryant, peering critically at his fingertip. 'I think it's starting to heal properly at last. I should think you're relieved.'

'Tell you the truth, it's never really troubled me,' he confessed. 'It were the wife sent me along. Said it looked unsightly and she weren't going out with me again till I did something about it. Not that we go out much, mind. Just Friday nights down the Rose and Crown, for the darts. I've played for years, but she's just decided to join in, and she's in the women's team,' he said, clearly proud of her. 'I couldn't mess that up because of my finger, now, could I?'

Anna smiled. 'Well, you're safe now, then. You can still go down to the Rose and Crown together on Fridays. It sounds like fun.'

He nodded. 'We enjoy it. Bit of light relief at the end of the week, 'specially in the winter. You ought to come along—you ever played darts?'

She laughed. 'Yes—I missed the board every time. I nearly put someone's eye out with one throw. I haven't tried since,' she admitted ruefully. 'Anyway, I can't get out easily because of Harry.'

Mr Bryant's eyes softened. 'He's a lovely little chap. Saw him the other day out for a walk with your mother, bless her. Dear little fellow. Gave me a great big smile, he did. Shame you haven't got a man to take care of you, my dear. I know it's none of my business, but a boy that age needs his mother, and I reckon you need him, too. Less hay fever that way.'

And he lifted his hand in farewell and stomped out of the surgery, leaving her laughing wryly. And she'd thought she'd fooled him!

Friday afternoon was her afternoon off, and she left the surgery at lunchtime without seeing Max. He was out on call, apparently, and so she went home with a strange, hollow feeling inside, changed out of her uniform and went round to see her mother.

Perceptive woman that she was, she took one look at her only daughter and pushed her into a chair. 'Stay here,' she ordered softly, took little Harry by the hand and led him off to find her husband.

Moments later she was back, walking straight up to Anna and engulfing her in a wordless hug.

All the fears she'd stifled for the past twelve hours or so welled up in a great hideous tide, and she buried her face in her mother's soft and comforting bosom and howled her eyes out. Finally, after what seemed like an age, she hiccuped to a halt, and her mother smoothed her hair one last time and handed her a fistful of tissues.

She blew her nose and wiped her cheeks, stifled another bout of weeping and watched as her mother bustled about with the kettle.

She made two mugs of tea, put them down in the middle of the table and pushed one towards Anna. 'Do you want to talk about it?' she asked gently.

Anna sniffed and tipped her head back, looking up at the ceiling for strength and inspiration. There was none to be found. 'He's dying,' she said flatly. 'Max. He's got lymphoma. That's why he left me.'

'Oh, my love...' Her mother's warm, capable hand

closed over hers, squeezing hard. 'Oh, darling, I am so sorry.'

The tears started again, and Anna dashed them away impatiently. 'He's in remission. He might be all right for years and years, but he won't stay. He won't listen to me—he says he'll think about staying till Suzanna comes back, but he won't stay after that, and he doesn't want Harry to know who he is, and I can't persuade him and I don't know what to do! I can't bear to lose him again...'

She dropped her head onto her arms, and sobbed helplessly, while her mother held her hand and murmured the sort of words she said to Harry when he fell and scraped his knees. Universal words, meaningless sounds that soothed and comforted and took away the pain.

Words she should have said to Max when he'd been lying in hospital, all alone.

She pushed herself up and gulped her tea, sniffing hard. 'He's so damn stubborn,' she said on a hiccuping sob. 'He just won't listen to me. It's my decision whether I can cope with it or not.'

'And can you?' her mother asked gently.

Anna sighed. 'I don't know. Better than I can cope with him leaving me, and not knowing if he was alive or dead—'

She broke off, pressing her fingers to her mouth to hold in the fear.

'How does he feel about you?' her mother asked.

She shrugged. 'He said he'd missed me. He said leaving was the hardest thing he'd ever done. He said he thought he must have misremembered how it was with me—'

She broke off, colouring, and wondered what her

mother would think if she realised she'd spent the night with him.

'And had he?' she asked softly.

Anna shook her head. 'No. We still...' She floundered to a halt, unsure how to phrase it, but her mother understood.

'Sometimes it's just right, I suppose. Your father and I met and fell headlong in love. There was no doubt, no question of waiting to be sure. We *were* sure, right from the first moment we set eyes on each other.'

She coloured softly and looked away. 'That's why we were married so quickly. Everyone thought it was because I was pregnant, but it was just that we couldn't stay away from each other, and it wasn't like it is these days. People didn't just live together—at least, not in the country.'

She smiled. 'So we were married, just eight weeks after we met, and thirty-four years later we're still here. I suppose we've been incredibly lucky. We've both got our health, we're happy, we've got a lovely daughter and a beautiful grandson—the only thing I would change is your happiness, and that's been something that's troubled me ever since Max came into your life.'

'You're very fortunate,' Anna told her wistfully. 'Treasure him. Not everyone gets the chance.'

Sarah Young swallowed hard and patted her daughter's hand. 'I know. I do.' She stood up, clearing away the cups—bustling to keep her emotions in check, Anna thought. She turned and gave Anna an over-bright smile. 'So how about giving me a hand to get lunch?'

*   *   *

Max drove slowly through the lanes, looking for Culvert Farm. He checked his directions again, and wondered if he'd passed that little turning or not.

He wasn't exactly concentrating. All he could think about was Anna, and how incredibly sweet it had been to lie in her arms last night. She wanted him to stay. He laughed wryly. If she only knew how easy it would be to do that, to give up being noble and let her share the uncertainty of the coming years.

But he couldn't, because of Harry. Oddly enough, if it hadn't been for the boy he might have stayed this time, but he couldn't trash the kid's life like that. What if he came out of remission and went downhill fast? It could happen. If he was on his own, nobody else would be affected and it wouldn't matter.

Still, she'd made a very tempting offer. Stay until Suzanna came back off maternity leave, she'd suggested, and make memories with her. It was unbelievably tempting—so tempting he thought he'd do it. Why not? They were both going to be hurt anyway. It might as well be worthwhile.

A bubble of something rose in his chest, and he realised it was happiness. It was the first time for five years—he almost hadn't recognised it. Yes, he'd stay, and make memories with her, and then he'd go, taking his memories with him to comfort him through the months and years ahead.

But he wouldn't think of that now. He'd concentrate on finding his patient, then going to see Anna and asking her to have dinner with him. Perhaps they'd go somewhere in the village, or in a nearby town. He'd ask if she had any preference.

Humming softly, he turned down the little lane he'd missed the first time, swung into the yard of Culvert Farm and cut the engine.

A man in overalls and boots was crossing the yard, and he smiled. 'Wonderful day,' he called.

The man nodded. 'You looking for David Bliss?'

'Yes—I'm the doctor.'

'I'm his son—he's inside. I'll take you in.'

He followed the man through the open doorway, past the sleeping collies that opened one eye and watched him warily, up the narrow winding cottage staircase to a bedroom.

'Father, Doctor's here,' the man said, and left them to it.

'Mr Bliss? I'm Dr Carter—I've taken over from Dr Korrel. I understand you've been having pain in your chest and you're a bit breathless. Is that right?'

The man heaved himself up the bed a little and nodded, puffing slightly from the effort. He looked congested, Max thought, his fingers a little swollen, his face round. His breathing seemed laboured, and a quick examination revealed all the symptoms of angina and congestive heart failure.

'Where do you feel the pain, and when?' he asked, checking his patient's chest with a stethoscope. It sounded like a soggy sponge.

'Up the middle, really. Sometimes down my arm a little, but not much. More into the armpit.'

Max nodded, sat him up and listened to the back of his chest, then took off the stethoscope and tucked it in his pocket.

'I think your heart's struggling a bit to keep your fluid levels right, and that's making it hurt periodically,' he told the elderly man. 'I'm going to give you some pills to take some of the fluid away from your lungs, and that should make you feel better quite quickly. You will find you need to pass water more often, though.'

He nodded. 'My sister's on them water tablets,' he said. 'Has been for years. Father was as well.'

'Perhaps it's something you all suffer from, then. Well, as you know, if it's kept under control it's nothing to worry about, but I want to put you on some pills for your heart as well, and I want you to try these. You pop one under your tongue if you have a pain, and if the pain goes, we'll know it's nothing to worry about, just a touch of angina. If the pain lingers or gets worse, I want to know straight away, all right?'

He went back out into the sunshine, found Mr Bliss's son and told him what he'd found, and then drove back to Wenham Market. There was no reply from Anna's house, but Jill Fraser stuck her head out of an upstairs window. 'She's at her mother's,' she said cheerfully. 'Did you have a good time last night?'

'Yes—thank you,' he said, a little taken aback. 'Were you babysitting?'

'That's right. Go and find her—you might have to go round the back, they'll probably be in the garden with a paddling pool in this lovely weather. We're just going to the beach.'

Max nodded, thanked her and drove down the lane, turning onto the gravel sweep in front of the Youngs' farmhouse. He rang the bell twice, and then one of the dogs bounded lazily up to him, barking a greeting, and he ruffled its ears and asked it where the others were.

It bounded back round the side of the house, and he followed a little hesitantly. He didn't like just walking in on them like that, but Jill had seemed to think it would be all right.

'Hello, anybody home?' he called, and the other dog

ambled up, too hot to bark or do anything more kinetic than wave its tail.

Anna appeared, looking a little surprised to see him, and he apologised.

'Your neighbour told me to come round the back,' he explained.

'That's fine. Come on in, I just wasn't expecting you. I thought you were out, doing calls. Harry's in the paddling pool.'

There was a splash and a shriek, and Harry came tearing round the side of the shrubs, dripping wet and laughing gleefully. He skidded to a halt and looked up at Max.

'Hello,' he said curiously. 'Have you come for tea? Grannie's just getting some.'

He looked at Anna, and she shrugged. 'It's up to you. We'd like you to join us—you know you're welcome.'

He hesitated. The boy was there, drawing him like a magnet, and yet this wasn't part of his plan.

'We've made lemon drizzle cake,' Harry confided, and that did it.

Max smiled wryly. 'Thank you, that sounds wonderful. I'd be delighted to stay.'

'You need shorts on,' Harry told him, and then ran off again. There was another splash, and a shriek from Grannie who was presumably soaked. Max chuckled and followed Anna round the shrubbery into the garden, his heart lighter than it had been for years.

Maybe this wouldn't be so hard, after all.

'Will you stay for supper?'

Max smiled at Mrs Young and shook his head. 'I don't think so. I have to go back for evening surgery in a minute. Actually, I was going to ask Anna if she wanted to join me for dinner.'

Anna's eyes met his searchingly. 'Dinner?' she said doubtfully. 'I just ate three slices of cake.'

He smiled. She always had loved cake. 'We could eat lightly—or just have a drink. It doesn't matter.'

'I'll have Harry,' her mother offered. 'He can stay the night with his grandparents. He enjoys that.'

'He was with Jill last night,' Anna said without thinking, and then coloured.

Her mother ignored her embarrassment. 'Well, that's all right,' she said. 'He loves coming here, it's like a second home, and we love having him. You have little enough social life, darling. You go out. You can always put him to bed before you go, if you're worried about not seeing him. It's not as if you've been at work all day today, is it?'

In the face of such common sense, Anna couldn't think of a single valid reason why she shouldn't go out with Max that night, whatever he had in mind. Perhaps he'd decided what he was going to do, and would tell her.

She felt a surge of adrenaline. If he was going to tell her he was leaving, surely he wouldn't have spent the entire afternoon with her and Harry, laughing and playing with his son, kicking balls around on the lawn and spreading sunblock on his nose and cheeks like a practised father.

'That would be lovely,' she said, without giving herself any more time to vacillate. 'Eight o'clock?'

He nodded. 'Maybe by then the cake will have worn off and you'll be able to eat,' he teased.

'On top of that lot?' She laughed. 'Hardly. I'll be like a house if I eat that much.'

He smiled indulgently. 'Don't hold back on my account. I like the new you. You were too skinny before.'

She coloured furiously, and he suddenly seemed to realise her mother was sitting in earshot, valiantly trying to pretend that she couldn't hear every word.

He cleared his throat and got to his feet. 'I'll see you at eight, then. Thank you for a lovely afternoon.'

She smiled up at him. 'You're welcome. See you later.'

She watched him go, then thought of that evening. Was he going to tell her that he'd decided to stay? Or had he stayed that afternoon just making memories, as she'd suggested, and was going to say goodbye that night? Only time would tell.

CHAPTER FIVE

'THIS is bliss,' Max said, stretching out luxuriously on the grass beside the river.

They were lying near a weeping willow, its branches hanging low over the water, and a cool breeze wafted over them, dispelling the heat of the day. Swans drifted in the current, paddling lazily to hold their positions, and there was the occasional splosh from the riverbank as a little vole or something plopped into the water.

It *was* bliss, but Anna was on edge. She wanted to know what he was thinking, and he didn't seem to be about to bring up the subject. Unable to help herself, she challenged him.

'Are you going?'

He opened his eyes and sat up slowly. 'Going?' he echoed. 'I'm not going anywhere—most particularly not until my food arrives.'

She rolled her eyes. 'You know what I mean. Are you going to stay and see out this locum job, or are you running away again?'

'Is that how you see it? Running away again?'

'Don't you?'

'Not really.' He gave a short, hollow laugh. 'I'm probably a fool, but I thought I'd stay for now.'

Relief washed over her like a tidal wave. 'I just wanted to know,' she said, trying to sound unmoved. 'And what about Harry? Will you see him—get to know him at all? You seemed to get on well today.'

He rolled onto his front and propped himself up on

his elbows, regarding her steadily. 'I don't know. I could easily fall for him. I think I probably have. I don't want to hurt him when I go—and I am going,' he said firmly. 'It's up to you whether I see him or not in the interim.'

She looked away, stifling her disappointment. One step at a time, she cautioned herself. 'I think you should see him, but maybe just as a friend, at least for now. I don't want him hurt either, and he will be if you tell him you're his father and then leave.'

He nodded. 'That's what I thought. So, in the meantime,' he asked softly, 'what are we going to do to make these memories of yours? Any particular fantasies you have in mind?'

Anything with you in it, she could have said, but she didn't. She didn't think it was a good idea to be too up-front—and, anyway, if she played her cards right, she could use this time together to get so far under his skin that he couldn't bear to leave them.

'Making love under a willow,' she said, her voice whisper-soft.

One eyebrow shot up. 'Not this one at this precise moment, I take it?' he said with a chuckle.

She looked around the crowded pub garden and shook her head with a smile. 'Not this one, and not now, no. But some time, somewhere.'

His eyes darkened. 'OK,' he agreed slowly. 'Anything else?'

She settled down on the grass, getting into the game. 'Oh—midnight skinny-dipping at the beach?'

His mouth twitched. 'Like prison food, do you?'

She laughed softly, then became wistful again. 'Waking up with you,' she said without a trace of a smile. 'I loved waking up with you.'

He looked away. Too close to home, she thought. 'What about you?' she asked. 'Any memories you want to make?'

'More than I care to think about,' he said gruffly, and rolled over and sat up, staring down into the slowly moving water. He propped his elbows on his knees, fisting one hand and wrapping the fingers of the other over it tightly. 'A picnic,' he said after an age. 'Going for a picnic on a perfect day—with Harry. Maybe going to the zoo? Walking in the countryside, by a river. Lying in on a Sunday and reading the papers. Fighting over the colour supplement. Making love in the shower.'

Five years ago they'd only had two Sundays together, and he'd been on call for one and she'd had a long-standing commitment on the Saturday night before the other, and so neither time had they been able to have a lie-in. Maybe this time, if she could persuade her mother to have Harry—?

'Number forty-two?'

'That's us,' Max said, getting to his feet and going over to the waitress to fetch the plates. 'Do you want to sit at a table, or can we manage here?' he asked her.

'Here,' she said without hesitation. 'Or nearer the river.'

'Those swans might get a bit too interested if you go nearer,' he warned, and so they stayed where they were, in the shelter of the willow, and ate their ham and prawn salad with fresh crusty rolls and creamy butter, washed down with ice-cold mineral water.

It was delicious—cool and light enough to eat even after pigging out on her mother's cake, and yet tasty and interesting.

'Lovely ham,' Max commented.

'It's wild boar ham, from a totally free-range herd. All the food here's organic. That's why I suggested it.'

He raised an enquiring brow. 'Have you gone organic, then?'

She shook her head. 'Not entirely. Wherever possible or reasonable, though. My father's an organic farmer now—has been for over ten years. He's doing much better than he was, because the demand is growing. The sheep are all grass fed without prophylactic medicines, and he raises geese and bronze turkeys for Christmas, again all organic and free range.'

'What about Mr Bryant? What does he do?'

'Oh, arable—all sprayed within an inch of its life. It's a problem, actually, because one of our fields is adjacent to one of his and we can't graze the ewes on it because of the spraying.'

'That's a bit of a pain. Is the field wasted?'

She shook her head. 'No. It's all right for the turkeys because he sows spring wheat, not winter wheat, so there's no spraying when we're growing them on. We keep trying to persuade him to grow something else there, but he's a bit resistant. Knows what he knows, and all that. He's very nice about it, but he's a nice man,' she added, remembering his remark about hay fever.

She picked up a cherry tomato in her fingers and ate it. 'So, what about you?' she asked. 'Do you still eat the most awful rubbish, like you did?'

He laughed. 'No, not really. I decided if I was going to fight this thing I ought to give my body the best possible chance, so I learned to cook and count grams of fat, and I eat tons of fresh fruit and veg, and I've cut down on meat now. I eat a lot of fish and chicken, pulses, that sort of thing, and virtually no packaged convenience foods. I like fresh ingredients.'

'Hence your fresh pasta last night.'

'Hence my fresh pasta every time I cook it.'

He put his plate down and met her eyes. 'Want to go and make some memories?' he asked softly.

She put her plate on his and stood up. 'Where are we going?'

'I don't know. My cottage? We could go for a walk down the lane to the river.'

She smiled. 'Is there a weeping willow?'

'No. There's a willow, but it's quite cheerful. Anyway, it's a bit muddy and there are lots of little bugs and things at night.'

So they went back to his cottage, and wandered down the lane hand in hand and found Max's cheerful willow, and sat on a fallen branch and talked until the light was fading.

Then they strolled back, arms wrapped round each other's waists, and in the kitchen they hesitated.

'Coffee?' Max offered.

She shook her head. 'Maybe later,' she murmured, summoning up her courage. Perhaps he didn't want her. Perhaps she was taking it for granted...

'Maybe,' he said softly, and drew her into his arms. 'I wouldn't have believed it was possible, but I think you're more beautiful now than you were before.'

Her cheeks warmed. 'You're just an old smoothie,' she said, flattered despite herself. 'You're just buttering me up so you can have your evil way with me.'

'Rumbled,' he said with a chuckle. 'Did it work?'

She smiled up at him. 'Oh, yes, it worked.'

They took Harry to the zoo on Sunday afternoon—after a morning spent building memories of squabbling over the colour supplement and making love in the shower. Harry adored his father, and it seemed it was mutual.

Excellent, she thought. If he gets in deep enough, he won't be able to walk away. They fed the llamas, oohed and aahed at the elephants and big cats, and giggled at the giraffe.

Then they went back to Anna's house and she cooked for Max, for a change, while he bathed Harry and got him ready for bed.

They came down more or less dry and looking so like each other it made her breath catch in her throat, and she thought she was going to cry again.

Fortunately the cat made a nuisance of itself and got on the worktop, and under cover of the diversion she got herself back under control. They ate their supper, a chicken casserole with baby new potatoes and tiny carrots, and then it was time for Harry to go to bed.

'Will you stay for coffee?' she asked him as Harry chased the cat into the sitting room.

'Do you want me to?'

She shrugged. 'It's up to you. It'll take me some time to put him to bed—we always read for a while. And…' She hesitated, not knowing quite how to put into words her reluctance to behave as they had in the privacy of his cottage with Harry in the house, but he read her mind again.

'Don't worry. I'll go. I don't want to make things awkward for you. I've had a wonderful weekend. Thank you.'

And without further ado, he bent forward, kissed her cheek circumspectly and ruffled Harry's hair on the way past.

''Night, sport. Be good. See you soon.'

''Night, Max,' Harry piped. 'See you soon, too.'

She caught a glimpse of his face as he went through the door, and his mouth was set in a bitter-sweet smile. And no wonder, she thought. Harry was the only child he would ever have—at least, she imagined so, unless he'd taken advantage of the sperm bank before his treatment had started. He hadn't talked about it, apart from telling her that there was no danger of pregnancy, and she didn't feel somehow that she could ask. It was rather a personal issue, after all, even with their history.

And what was their history? she wondered sadly. A wild and hot affair five years ago and, judging by the way their current relationship was shaping up, another hot and wild affair now, interspersed with trips to the zoo and the beach. No wonder she didn't feel she could ask him about the sperm bank. She really didn't know him at all.

She sighed and ruffled Harry's hair. 'Shall we go and find a story?' she asked.

'Can we have Peter Rabbit?'

'Again?' she teased.

'Or Tom Kitten.'

The old Beatrix Potter books from her childhood were his favourites, to her surprise. All the modern, highly coloured books left him cold. He much preferred the simple, beautifully illustrated animal fantasies that she had enjoyed so much as a child.

'We'll go and look, shall we?' she said, and five minutes later he was curled up in the crook of her arm, laughing at the antics of Tom Kitten and his sisters. Ten minutes later, he was asleep.

Max could have stayed. He could have joined in story time, but, in fact, Anna was glad he'd gone home. She needed a breathing space, time to think, time to come to terms with Thursday night's revelation. It was only Sunday, and she'd hardly been out of his sight the entire time.

She needed time alone, and she imagined he did, too.

So much had happened, and yet nothing had changed.

He was still leaving, and Harry still didn't have a father, and she was going to be alone again.

The thought was unbearable.

He was getting in too deep. Spending just about every waking minute since Thursday—and many sleeping ones—with Annie, that had been a mistake. And as for Harry, he thought the child could easily break his heart.

He was a darling, with a highly developed sense of fun and an insatiable curiosity. He'd never stopped asking questions the whole time they'd been at the zoo, and Max began to understand why people found their much-loved children so exhausting. They seemed to run on some kind of rocket fuel, but fortunately, like rockets, after a while they fizzled out and went quiet, at least for a while.

He wondered what story Annie had read him, and found himself driving past at a quarter to midnight to see if she still had her bedroom light on.

She didn't, but there was a faint glow that probably came from the landing. He wanted to stay there, parked outside, protecting them like some kind of guardian angel.

That was when he realised he was in over his head.

For the next few days, they gave each other space. It wasn't easy for either of them, and yet they both seemed to need it, and by some unspoken mutual agreement they chatted at work, and then went their separate ways.

Max, particularly, wondered if it had all been a big mistake and if he should have gone when he'd had the chance. He'd told her now, though, that he would stay for a while, and stay he would, even though it was killing him.

Instead of beating himself over the head with it, though, he concentrated on his patients. There was plenty to do. It was a busy practice, and as she'd predicted it wasn't long before Jill Fraser, Anna's neighbour, brought one of her children in.

'This is Will,' she said, sitting down with the screaming baby on her lap. 'I think he's got another ear infection.'

'Oh, dear.' Max slid his chair forward and felt the baby's head, and it was hot. That might have been because he was crying, or because he had a fever. 'Could I look in his ear?' he asked, and directed Jill to turn his head to one side and hold it firmly against her front.

She had obviously done it before, probably numerous times with her three children over the years. She had that resigned look of the long-suffering mother, and Max wondered if she was all right herself, or if she was suffering from stress.

'I just want to check the ear with another device,' he explained. 'It tests the mobility of the middle ear— if there's liquid in there, or pus, it will tell me because that will make the whole mechanism less mobile. The eardrum becomes stiff, the little bones inside don't move properly, and that sort of thing.'

'Does it hurt?' she asked.

He shook his head. 'No, it doesn't hurt—it's just a

little probe that seals in the ear, attached to this thing like a gun.'

'Oh, good,' Jill said with a laugh. 'Are you going to shoot him?'

Max smiled. 'Been a bit rough, has it, over the last few days?'

'A bit?' Her smile wobbled, and she turned away. 'You could say that. It wouldn't be so bad if I had someone to share it, but I don't, not since Mick walked out yet again.'

Definitely stressed, Max thought. 'Was this recently?' he asked, fitting the right-sized probe in the tympanometer and placing it in the child's ear. Within a second he had his result—the sound returning to the machine was diminished, which meant the child's ear was full of fluid.

'Two months ago,' Jill replied, mechanically stroking the baby's head to soothe him. 'That was the third time he left. I won't have him back again. It's when they come and go it's so hard. You go through all the grieving for the relationship, and then they come back, and then they go, and you do the grieving again but this time there's hope, and then they come back, and go—it's hell. I wish he'd just go and stay gone.'

Max sat back in the chair and studied her body language. She was dealing with the baby all right, but she was tense, her shoulders hunched, her neck stiff, and it was his bet that if she relaxed she'd howl her eyes out—and the baby, not unnaturally, was picking up on it.

'Let me see the little fellow,' he said, reaching out for the child. The baby relaxed against him almost instantly, sensing his calm presence even though he was a total stranger, and Jill sighed as the noise diminished to a dull sniffle.

'Do you want to make an appointment to come and see me on your own for a chat?' he asked. 'I think you're very stressed, and maybe I can do something to help you.'

'Put me on tranks, you mean?' she said sceptically. 'No, thanks.'

'Not tranquillisers, necessarily. I don't like them any more than you do, but there are other things. Have you tried St John's wort? It's a relation of rose of Sharon. It's brilliant for TATT—tired all the time. It happens to so many people we've even given it a name! Unfortunately, I can't prescribe it, because it's not a recognised remedy, being herbal, and it's not regulated in the same way, but if you can afford it, it may well help you.'

'I'll try it. It certainly sounds like me.'

'Now, getting back to the baby for a minute, he's definitely got fluid in his ear, and he might have a condition called glue ear, when they get sticky gunk in the ear all the time. If so, he might need to be referred to a specialist. I'll give him something to take, and you need to give him paracetamol syrup, but I don't want to give him antibiotics because these ear bugs get very resistant and most of the time the body can sort itself out if you give it long enough. OK?'

She nodded.

'Now, about you. Try the St John's wort, and come back to see me if it's not working or if you can't wait that long—it might take a week or so to kick in. Be patient. And if you want to chat, just come in. OK? I'll fit you in.'

'Thanks.' She smiled, a fragile smile that he sensed

would dissolve into tears at the slightest provocation, and took her baby off his lap while he printed out the prescription and handed it to her.

'Take care,' he said, and she nodded and left.

'I wish he'd just go and stay gone.'

Max closed his eyes. Was he doing the same thing to Anna? And to himself?

'Oh, hell's teeth,' he sighed, and pressed his buzzer for the next patient.

He saw Anna later, and found a quiet moment to ask her about Jill. 'Do you think she's depressed and stressed out any more than normal? She brought the baby in with an ear infection and I thought she seemed very flat.'

'I noticed that,' Anna said thoughtfully. 'I was going to keep an eye on her.'

'Would you? I'd be grateful. What's her financial situation like? I've recommended she takes St John's wort, but, of course, I can't prescribe it and it isn't cheap.'

'Oh, Mick's more than generous,' Anna said drily. 'He just won't give them his time. Too busy doing what he wants to do—which most of the time seems to be other women. But, no, she's not that short of money, I don't think.'

Max nodded, and wondered why a man married to an attractive, pleasant woman like Jill Fraser would need to play the field. A flaw in himself, he thought, but the end result was the same, possibly, no matter why he left.

Was he himself behaving as badly as that? He was doing it for their sakes, though.

'Penny for them,' Anna murmured.

He gave a short laugh. 'Not a chance.' He suddenly

realised how much he'd missed her in the past few days
and nights. 'I don't suppose you could find a babysitter,
could you?'

'Tonight?'

He shrugged. 'If possible, but if not then tomorrow?'

She was silent for a moment, then she smiled sadly.
'OK. I'll ask my parents. Do you want him to stay
overnight?'

Their eyes met, and heat seared between them. 'It's
up to you,' he said, putting the ball back in her court.
'I thought, as it's so hot, we might go swimming in the
sea tonight.'

'At midnight?' she asked, and he could see the anticipation in her eyes.

'Uh-huh.'

She swallowed. 'I'll ask. I'm just going round there
for lunch. I'll tell you later.'

He watched her go, anticipation tightening his gut,
and wondered if he was insane to stay, to make her
memories, to indulge both of them in this lunatic folly.

Probably, but it was beyond him to stop. He didn't
care how much it hurt later. He'd deal with it then. For
now, he wanted to be with her every minute of every
day.

Making memories.

It was a gorgeous night. They found a deserted stretch
of beach, with sand at the waterline and pebbles at high
water, and near the top of the sand Max built a little
campfire with driftwood and they sat beside it, staring
out over the moonlit sea.

The light gleamed on the lazy swell, and the soft
rush of the breaking waves lulled their senses. It was

hypnotic, enchanting and utterly romantic, and Anna wanted to stay there with him for ever.

'Fancy a walk?' Max asked, and she nodded.

'Can do. Are we going far?'

'I doubt it.'

She stood up, brushing sand off her bottom, then took off her shoes and rolled up the hems of her jeans. Max did the same, and then, arm in arm, they strolled along the waterline, gasping with laughter every now and then as a more adventurous wave curled coldly around their ankles.

Then one particularly big wave came and soaked them to the knees, and Anna screamed and ran up the beach, Max in hot pursuit.

He chased her back past their little campfire, down towards a breakwater, and when she reached it she was too slow to climb over.

'Got you,' he said victoriously, and turned her, laughing, into his arms.

'That's cheating—I had to stop,' she protested, but it was a token protest and she was happy to be caught—especially when he silenced her by the simple expedient of cutting off her air supply with a kiss.

The resistance and laughter drained out of her, and she leant into his arms, slid her hands round and tucked them in the back pockets of his jeans and groaned softly with pleasure. It seemed like days since he'd kissed her, and with the sighing of the surf in the background, the utter peace and tranquillity of the night, the vast openness of the sea beside them, she couldn't have designed a more perfect setting.

His mouth was gentle, coaxing, sipping and teasing at her lips, trailing hot, open-mouthed kisses over her throat and down the open V of her blouse.

He opened first one button, then the next, his lips following his hands to kiss every inch of skin as it was revealed. She felt the cool salt air on her skin, the hot moisture of his tongue followed by the cooling breeze, and wondered how it was possible for sensation to be so heightened by the romance of the night.

Because it *was* heightened, without question. Unbearably heightened, every sense alert, aware, more receptive than ever before.

There was no sound apart from the soft rush of the sea and their breathy sighs, their bodies caressed by the cool fingers of night air whispering over their skin. They were utterly alone, wrapped in a private world, and they could have been a hundred miles from civilisation, not just a matter of minutes.

He lifted his head and rested it against hers, his breathing ragged. His fingers fumbled to do up her buttons, and, regretfully, she moved to help him. It was common sense. They weren't miles from anywhere, and anyone could have walked along the beach and found them.

'Do you want your swim, or do you want to go home?' he asked softly.

'Swim,' she said instantly. 'Are we going to be daring?'

He chuckled. 'Why not? We can stay in the water if anyone comes along. Anything to help your fantasies along.'

They looked around, then stripped off their clothes and ran headlong into the sea, gasping with shocked laughter as they hit the water. Once they were in it was wonderful, the sea caressing them like liquid velvet, rocking them gently in the slow, languid swell.

They kissed again, just affectionate, loving touches

in the silvering moonlight, and then hand in hand they walked out of the sea, water streaming from their skin and leaving silver trails in the sand. They dressed, sandy legs and all, and limped and picked their way over the stones to the car park.

Anna didn't bother with her shoes. Instead, she brushed off the loose sand, swung her feet in and left them to dry while Max, properly shod again, drove them home.

They arrived back at his cottage at after one, showered off the salt and sand and went to bed, their hair still damp, too impatient to dry it properly. It had been days since they'd been alone, and their hunger had been sharpened by anticipation.

Anna took everything he had to offer, and in return she gave him everything she had to give, and later, lying quietly and drowsing in the still of the night, she thought back over the evening.

It was a beautiful memory. She would file it away carefully, smoothed flat and placed with infinite care where she could view it on demand, and she would treasure it.

CHAPTER SIX

As THE days turned to weeks, almost as many weeks as they'd had before, Anna grew to know and love Max even more. They seemed so in tune with each other that it was uncanny, and without the threat to his future, life would have been perfect.

Oddly it wasn't the threat of his death that troubled her. More that he would go, and that she would lose such time as he did have left. And the frustrating thing was that it could, and probably would, be years and years. It was entirely possible that he would outlive her, and yet she seemed unable to persuade him to stay longer than he had agreed, or to tell Harry who he was.

'What about your parents?' she said one day, as they were sitting in the garden of his cottage, staring out over the countryside and sipping wine. 'Have you told them about Harry?'

He looked at her as if she had lost her mind. 'My parents? No, of course I haven't told them! What would I tell them?'

Anna laughed incredulously. 'That you have a son? Max, Harry's their grandson, a part of you that will live on. Don't you think they have a right to know about him? And what about Harry? Don't you think he's entitled to their love and friendship as he grows older? And what about uncles and aunts and cousins? It's not just you you're depriving him of, Max. It's your entire family. Do you really think that's fair?'

He looked away, his face drawn into troubled lines.

'I don't know. I don't know what to do, Annie,' he confessed wearily. 'Part of me wants to pretend this isn't happening, and just ignore it. Another part insists on staring it in the face.' He turned to her, his eyes unshuttered for once, open and revealing. 'I love you. Whatever happens, I want you to know that.'

She sighed harshly round the lump in her throat. 'This sounds like another of your ''I'm doing for your own good'' speeches, Max. Maybe *I* want to be the judge of what's good for me and Harry. Especially Harry. He's always talking about not having a father.'

Max looked shocked. 'What have you told him? I didn't even think, but I suppose he must wonder because his friends have fathers. So what did you say?'

She lifted her shoulders in a quick shrug. 'I told him that I loved his father very much but he had to go away. He wants to know when he's coming back, and I keep telling him never. He asked again the other day.'

He froze, shock written on his face. 'What did you tell him?' he demanded hoarsely.

'The same. What could I tell him?' she asked bitterly. 'That he was here—that he'd already met his father and liked him? That his father loved him but wasn't man enough to deal with it?'

'That's not true!' he protested. 'You know that's not true.'

'Isn't it?'

She stood up and brushed down her skirt. 'I'm going home. Don't bother to come. I'll walk.'

And she turned on her heel and left him.

Max contemplated finishing the bottle of wine but thought better of it. Instead, he sat staring blankly out over the darkening countryside, considering what Anna had said and wrestling with his conscience. Finally coming to a conclusion, he stood up, carried his glass inside and dumped it in the sink, picked up his car keys and headed north, out along the A14 to Cambridge.

He arrived at his parents' house at something after ten, and let himself in through the back door. His parents were in the kitchen, feeding the cat, loading the dishwasher—doing all the usual family chores before bedtime—and they took one look at him and froze.

'I've got something to tell you,' he said, and the glass slid out of his mother's fingers and shattered all over the floor.

He dredged up a smile. 'Not that. I'm still in remission. It's something else—something I should have told you weeks ago.' He looked around restlessly, unsure how to go on, but his parents were quicker.

'Better get this glass cleared up while the kettle boils,' his father said practically. 'Max, hold the cat. Clare, mind your feet, darling. Just stand still.' He whisked the broom around her, then ran a wet cloth over the floor to pick up any tiny bits. Max shut the cat out and made coffee while his mother posted the last of the dishes into the machine.

'Right,' Henry Carter said, dusting off his hands. 'Let's go and sit down somewhere comfortable while you get whatever this is off your chest.'

Bless him, Max thought. He'd been a tower of strength through his illness. Maybe he could see a way through this.

They sat down, his parents watching him expectantly, and because there was no subtle way to do this, no easy way into the conversation, he said bluntly, 'I've got a son. He's called Harry, he's four years old and he doesn't know I'm his father.'

Shock held them motionless for ages, and then the questions started. When? How? Why hadn't he known? When did he find out?

And then the one he was dreading.

'When can we meet him?' his mother asked, on the edge of her seat, her face expectant and excited.

'You can't,' he said flatly. 'I'm not going to tell him who I am. It's not fair—in case anything happens.'

Of course, they went through all the arguments Anna had been through, and he gave them all the same replies until he began to feel like a programmed robot. Press button A to start, he thought impatiently, and stood up.

'Listen, I only told you because I thought you ought to know. If anything happens to me, I want you to contact Anna. I'll make sure you always have her correct address, and I'll keep you up to date with photos of Harry and so on, but I'm leaving Wenham Market as soon as my contract is up, and I won't be back. All communication with her will be by letter, through solicitors. All right?'

His mother burst into tears, his father stood up and gave her shoulder an agitated pat, before coming over to him and standing in front of him, toe to toe.

'Don't you think Harry has a right to his father?' he asked quietly. 'How would you have felt if I'd had an illness and cut you out of my life? Wouldn't you rather have done the things we did when you were a little boy? Gone fishing, kicked footballs, lain awake all night in the woods, looking for badgers—wouldn't you rather have had that than known nothing about me? Even if it meant you had to lose me, wouldn't it have been better to have had that first?'

Max looked down. The floor swam in front of his eyes, and he blinked. 'It's not the same.'

'How is it not the same? Except that you already have four years to make up for?'

'I want to meet him,' his mother pleaded from the sofa. 'Max, please—can't you bring him over? You don't have to tell him who you are—just invite them both here for lunch on Sunday, and we won't say anything, I promise. Just let us meet him—' She broke off, struggling with her composure again, and Max gave a short sigh.

'Dammit, Mother, don't cry,' he said gruffly. 'This is hard enough.' His voice cracked, and he went out to the kitchen and put the kettle on again to give himself something to do. The cat attacked his shoelaces, and he picked her up and tickled her chin. 'You're just like Anna's cat,' he told her. 'Wicked and into everything.'

She purred and butted his chin, and he hugged her and wished he could settle down in one place and maybe have a cat of his own—something on which to lavish all the love and devotion in him that was going to waste.

His mother came up behind him and slipped her arms round his waist. 'I'm sorry,' she said in a rather damp voice. 'I didn't mean to nag you. I know it has to be your decision, but perhaps you could think about it? Or maybe we could pop in to visit you and they could be there, almost by accident?'

'That might be better,' he conceded gruffly. 'I'm not just trying to be awkward, Mum. I feel the future's so uncertain I can't bear to expose him to it. It seems cruel.'

'And what does Anna think?'

He sighed. 'Anna agrees with you.'

He felt his mother's lips press lightly against his shoulder, and a lump formed in his throat.

'You must do what you think is best. Just let us know. Now, are you going to stay the night and drive back in the morning, or do you want another drink before you go?'

'I'll stay—if I may? I'm feeling pretty tired.' Too many nights with Annie, he thought sadly, filling up her memory banks...

Anna felt guilty. She'd stormed out without giving Max a chance to discuss it, accused him of not being man enough to deal with what was after all an incredibly painful and sensitive issue, and now she felt guilty.

Who was she to judge Max? She'd made mistakes with Harry. Every parent did. Maybe Max was no different. Whatever, she'd been unfair, and she couldn't sleep.

Because she'd planned to spend the evening with Max, Harry was staying with her mother, and so she didn't have to worry about him. She got out of bed and dressed quickly in her jeans and a sweater against the chilly night, and ran out to her car. She'd go round and see him and apologise, and then maybe stay the night.

If he forgave her.

The house was in darkness. It was after midnight, so it wasn't surprising, but his car wasn't on the drive, and she knew he wasn't on call.

A terrible cold fear crawled over her, seeping into her bones and filling her with a hideous dread.

'No!' she whispered. 'Not again. Max, no!'

She threw the door open and ran round the bonnet, hammering on his front door with her fists. 'Max!' she screamed. 'Max! Wake up. Open the door! Open the door!'

She slid to the step, her face against the cool wood burning with emotion and anxiety. She lifted her fist again and dropped it feebly against the door, a sob rising in her throat. 'Max? Please, Max, no...'

It was her fault. She'd driven him away, pushed him too hard, made an already difficult situation intolerable for him, and so he'd left her, gone away without a word.

'You promised,' she wept brokenly. 'You promised to tell me...'

She pounded the door again. 'Max! Damn you, answer the door!'

A light came on down the lane, in the neighbouring cottage a few hundred yards away. She saw a curtain twitch, and bit her lip. She had to live in this village. She couldn't be found weeping and ranting on his doorstep.

Mustering the last remnants of her common sense, she struggled to her feet and climbed back into the car. She couldn't drive away, though. She couldn't see, and the faster she blinked, the faster she misted up again.

'Oh, hell,' she mumbled, scrubbing her eyes with a tissue. 'Max, you promised...'

She gave up fighting, folded her arms over the steering-wheel and wept until she was too exhausted to move. Eventually, as the sky lightened in the east and the birds began to stir, she fell into an uneasy and troubled sleep.

She was woken by the car door opening, and Max's voice anxiously rousing her.

'Annie? Are you all right? What's wrong? Dear God, my love, what is it?'

He was here! He hadn't left—or if he had, he'd come back! And he'd called her his love. She sat up stiffly and met his troubled eyes. 'I thought you'd gone,' she said simply.

Max was gutted. He looked at her, so dear, so precious, at the grief in her face and the pain in her eyes, and he dragged her from the car and crushed her to his chest.

'Silly girl, of course I haven't gone!' he said roughly. 'I've been with my parents—I stayed the night. I've just come back to shower and change for work.'

'I couldn't believe it,' she told him, staring incredulously at him, touching his face as if to make sure he was real. 'I thought you'd left again without telling me, and you promised, but I was unfair to you—that's why I came back, to apologise, and you weren't here...' She hiccuped to a halt, and Max hugged her again, guilt stabbing through him.

'I'm sorry,' he whispered into her hair. 'You weren't unfair, you were right. I went to tell my parents about Harry.'

Her head snapped up and her eyes locked with his. 'And?' she said hopefully.

He sighed. 'They want to meet him.'

'That's wonderful,' she said softly. 'Oh, Max, that's wonderful—'

'I still don't want him to know—not yet, at least.' He heard that last qualifying remark, and wondered if Annie had noticed it.

'Not yet?' she echoed. 'But maybe—later?'

Damn. 'Slip of the tongue,' he told her, watching the hope die in her eyes and hating himself. 'Annie, don't.

I've had all I can deal with for now, and you have, too. Come inside—I need you. I missed you last night.'

'I missed you, too. I always miss you.'

He hugged her, unable to speak, and once through the door he drew her into his arms and kissed her hungrily. He didn't want to think any more, didn't want to ponder on the right course of action. He just wanted to hold her, to love her, to lose himself in her sweet warmth and let her love wash over him.

'Where's Harry?' he asked softly.

'With my parents. He's been there for the night.'

He remembered now. It seemed so long ago. He'd sat up with his parents, talking to them, until nearly one, and it was only six now. He held out his hand, and she took it, and wordlessly he led her upstairs to his bedroom and took her in his arms again.

'We'll be late,' she protested half-heartedly.

'No, we won't. I promise.'

He lied. She left him in the shower and rushed home, and they arrived almost simultaneously in their separate cars a scant two minutes late.

'Well, we almost made it,' he said with a wry smile, and she laughed softly and disappeared to collect her notes.

He checked his messages, scooped up his notes and went into his consulting room. His parents had been thrilled about Harry, he thought, and he was sure it was because they'd thought he'd never have another chance. He'd taken advantage of the sperm bank facilities—just in case, by a miracle, he should be cured and meet up with Annie again—but he hadn't held out much hope, and nor had his parents.

Funny, until Annie had pointed it out it had never

occurred to him that he was cheating them of their grandson.

He'd have to set up an impromptu get-together—a casual drop-in that gave them all a chance to meet without ceremony. Perhaps if they arrived just as he was taking Annie and Harry out for the day. They could join in...

Hmm. Interesting thought. He picked up the first set of patient notes, scanned them briefly and pressed the buzzer. He'd have to see what they were all doing this weekend, perhaps.

He soon forgot about his parents and Harry. It was a busy morning, made more hectic by a number of patients who came to see him with a whole list of things wrong with them.

'While I'm here, Doctor...' It was becoming an oft-repeated remark that was threatening to mess up his schedules beyond redemption.

Then Valerie Hawkshead was brought in by her husband as an emergency. They had been driving through town, and she'd had a seizure in the car. Could he see her?

He could. He was puzzled, and concerned. She'd come in two or three weeks ago and had had an urgent referral to a neurologist, once he'd dismissed any other obvious cause of her forgetfulness and headaches. She'd been sent back to him as suffering from depression with retardation, and needing drug therapy to alleviate this.

Unhappy with the diagnosis, he'd given her something suitable and was following her up regularly. This, though, was totally out of the blue, and threw a whole different light on the situation.

It was also potentially much more serious, he felt, and his unease grew when he saw her.

She was depressed, listless, her eyes seemed unfocussed and she had clearly gone downhill drastically. She was also suffering from a blinding headache, and needed urgent hospital assessment.

'I want her to go back to the hospital for a scan,' he told her husband. 'I'm not happy. This is not what I would have expected, and I think we need to find out what's caused it and why. I think it's perhaps a little bit more complicated than we'd all anticipated.'

He wrote a letter, handed it to them and asked them to go straight to the hospital radiology department. If, as he suspected, they found a brain tumour, and provided they were able to remove it successfully, she might find all her symptoms resolved themselves.

If not—well, if not, it could be terminal.

Assuming he was correct, of course. There was always a chance that he was mistaken, but he feared not. There was still the possibility of Creutzfeldt-Jakob disease—CJD, or mad cow disease as it was commonly and mistakenly called—or syphilis in a late stage. He couldn't tell, and there was no future in speculating.

That the hospital would admit her he was sure. He wondered how her family would cope, and how she would progress, and not for the first time he was frustrated that he would be unlikely to see their story through to the end.

The lack of continuity in patient care distressed him—so many times he picked up things that had a long-term treatment plan, and had to hand the patients over before he'd seen it through. It was frustrating, and it was also professionally undesirable because he was failing to build up a picture of many treatments that might help with future cases.

There was an answer, of course. Annie was pushing him towards it, but he didn't feel it was fair to his patients. What if he came out of remission and had to go for treatment, and was off for some weeks or months? Was it fair to expect patients to have to make do with a locum under those circumstances?

And, anyway, he thought drily, no practice in its right mind would take him on, knowing he had lymphoma. It was too risky, too uncertain a future to gamble on.

Whatever.

He pressed the buzzer for his next patient, suddenly aware that he'd been staring into space and had a queue of patients still to see.

Lack of sleep and too much emotion, he thought tiredly. Perhaps tonight he'd go round and visit Annie and Harry, and just sit and chat for a while, then go home for an early night.

He must remember to ask how Jill Fraser was getting on, on the subject of continuity and follow-up. Perhaps he'd even pop in to see her.

The doorbell rang, and Anna dusted her hands on her apron and followed Harry down the hall.

'Hello, sunshine,' Max said to the child, then looked up at her and smiled.

The sun came out in her heart, and she smiled back, holding the door wide. 'Come on in. We're still not ready—Harry's been helping me.'

He ran a laughing eye over her flour-spattered form, and grinned. 'Is it safe to eat?' he asked under his breath, and she laughed.

'Of course. It's going to be good, isn't it, Harry?'

Harry nodded. 'I put the eyes in,' he informed Max.

His eyebrows shot up, and Anna laughed again. 'In the gingerbread men. Nothing ghastly, don't worry. I'm not doing culinary experiments.'

'I'm relieved to hear it. Listen, I'm just going to pop in and have a chat to Jill for a moment, OK? I won't be long. Put the kettle on, I'm dying of thirst.'

He kissed her floury cheek and went out again, and she closed the door and went back to the kitchen to finish the preparations. They were having a barbecue, with chicken breasts cut into chunks and skewered with peppers, tiny onions and cherry tomatoes, and organic sausages in buns with fried onions, and loads of salad, the gingerbread men to follow.

Assuming they ever got into the oven.

'Harry, darling, that's enough buttons. Let's cook them now.' She slipped the tray into the oven, Harry standing well back as instructed, and then she told him he could sit down opposite the oven door and watch for them to go nicely brown.

'They're brown, Mummy,' he called excitedly almost before she was out of the kitchen.

'Harry, they can't be. Give them five minutes. Look—see the clock? See this long hand? When it gets to here, look again. All right?'

He nodded, and watched the clock unblinkingly. Every time she came back into the kitchen for something else, he was still in the same position, until in the end he called her again.

'They're brown now,' he yelled, and she went back in and opened the oven door.

'Not quite. Watch the hand to here,' she said, and then the doorbell rang again.

Harry pelted down the hall and struggled to reach the lock, and she took the safety catch off the top and opened it to let Max in.

'How is she?' she asked, following Harry slowly down the hall.

'Better, she thinks. I suspect it's as much because someone noticed as it is the St John's wort, but it is supposed to be very good. She certainly seems more cheerful and on top of things, but that might be because the baby's better.'

'Are you here for the evening now?' she asked with a smile.

'Yes. Come here.' He glanced down the hall at Harry, glued to the clock, and propelled her into the sitting room.

'They're ready,' Harry yelled, and Max laughed softly and kissed her anyway, just briefly.

'Later,' she promised, and then there was a scream from the kitchen and Max dropped her and sprinted down the hall.

She ran after him, to find him holding Harry screaming over the sink, cold water already running over his arm. There was a thin white line across his forearm— from the edge of the oven, she imagined—and guilt savaged her.

'What were you doing, darling?' she asked, soothing his brow and hugging him.

'They were ready,' he sobbed. 'I just wanted to take them out before they got burnted.'

'I'll take them out. You stay there with Max and let that cool down.'

She opened the oven, and still the biscuits were hardly cooked. But she'd had enough of his obsessive watching, and they would cook a moment longer on the oven tray. She pulled it out, put it out of Harry's reach and turned the oven off.

'Right. Leave them alone. They're for pudding, understand? Later.'

He nodded miserably, perched on the draining-board with Max holding his arm firmly but gently under the water. 'I just di'n't want them to get burnted,' he said again, and buried his face in her shoulder.

'I think it's all right. Have you got anything to put on it?' Max asked.

'Aloe vera—that's it there,' she said, pointing to a spiky succulent on the window sill. 'Just break a piece off and slice it up the middle, but mind the spikes at the sides.'

'What do you do with it then?' he asked, slicing with her vegetable knife.

'Tape it on for the night. By tomorrow it won't hurt and will almost have cleared up. It's a bit slimy, but it works wonders.'

She dried Harry's arm, and then taped the piece of juicy leaf in place. 'There,' she said with satisfaction. 'Now, let's go and start the barbecue before anything else happens.'

'Want a gingerbread man,' Harry said petulantly.

'No, they're hot, you'll burn your tongue and I can't stick aloe vera on that. Anyway, they're for pudding.'

They went outside, just in time to see the cat legging it down the garden with a string of sausages in tow.

'Oh, Felix, you horrible cat!' she wailed.

It was too much for Max. He leant back against the fence and laughed till his sides ached.

'Just for that you can starve,' Anna said repressively.

'I could nip to the shop for some burgers,' he offered.

'They're shut. Don't worry, I've got more in the freezer. I swear, one day I'm going to skin that cat.'

'A likely story,' Max said mildly, settling down in one of her garden chairs in the shade of the apple tree. 'This is such a pretty garden,' he murmured, looking round.

She glanced at it, and wondered if he could see the years of work that had gone into rescuing it from dereliction. Not that she'd done it alone, or the house. Her father and mother had been wonderful, in between telling her she was mad and ought to live with them instead of buying her own place, but she'd wanted privacy and a little emotional distance, and most of the time she was sure she'd done the right thing.

She found more sausages, and they cooked them and the chicken kebabs when the coals were hot, and then they had Harry's over-buttoned and slightly under-done gingerbread men for pudding with a dollop of organic ice cream which was the wickedest thing she'd ever tasted.

'This can't be healthy,' Max remarked, scraping the last trace from his bowl.

She laughed. 'Who said anything about healthy? It's stuffed with cholesterol and calories. It's just organic— it's not poisoned with sprays and chemicals and hormones and antibiotics. It doesn't mean it can't be wicked.'

'I want more,' Harry announced, but she shook her head.

'You've had more than enough to eat, young man. It's time for your bath and bed—you're late, and you've had too many nights with Grannie recently.'

'Want Max to bath me,' he said.

'Then ask nicely,' Max told him, firmly but gently.

'Please, will you bath me?' he asked him, and Max, only too willing by the look on his face, took his son by the hand and led him into the house, while Anna cleared up the dishes, washed up and indulged herself in a little sentimental cry.

Another memory, she thought.

Max had forgotten how easy it was to get wet, bathing young children. He hadn't spent all that much time with his nephews and nieces recently, but it all came flooding back, as it were.

I blame it on the mother, he thought wryly, getting another soaking from the water-pistol. Giving up, he wrestled it from the child, chucked it into the basin and pushed his sleeves up further.

'Right, hairwash and out,' he said, and laid the child back to wet his hair. He shampooed it carefully, laid him down again to rinse it and once more marvelled at how like his nephew Thomas Harry was.

A great wave of love washed over him, and he lifted the boy out, wrapped him in a towel and sat down on the lid of the loo seat to dry him. He squirmed and giggled and tried to get away, but Max managed to pin him down until he'd tickled him dry all over, and then he chased him along the corridor to his bedroom, bribed him into his pyjamas with the promise of an extra-long story, then settled down at the head of the bed, Harry tucked under his arm and a book in his hand.

That was how Anna found them an hour later, both fast asleep.

She woke Max gently, and he blinked and shifted carefully away from Harry, easing off the bed without disturbing him.

He needn't have worried. Harry rolled over, snuggling down under the quilt with a little sleepy noise, and they went downstairs.

They didn't talk for fear of disturbing him, but Max was glad of the silence. To be honest, he didn't think he could speak. Emotion was welling up in him, and when they reached the sitting room, as if she understood exactly what he felt, Anna opened her arms and hugged him.

'You don't have to go,' she reminded him. 'You could be part of this.'

He swallowed hard. 'Don't, please. Not tonight. Just hold me.'

So she held him, her hands tracing lazy circles on his back, and he dropped his head into the curve of her neck and let the soothing touch wash over him.

She was right. He could stay—but at what cost to them? And could he really ask them to pay the price?

CHAPTER SEVEN

'ABOUT my parents,' Max said the following day.

They were sitting in the tiny bit of garden at the back of the practice, perched on the wall in the sunshine, taking a well-earned rest. 'What about your parents?' Anna asked, blowing the steam off the top of her coffee.

'How about you and Harry coming to my place on Sunday for tea in the garden, and they can just "drop in", as it were, in passing?'

Anna sensed that it was a huge step forwards for Max, one he was taking reluctantly for the sake of his parents. 'Sounds fine,' she told him, concentrating on her coffee so he wouldn't see how pleased she was. 'What time do you want us? And do you want help with the tea?'

He grinned wryly. 'I was going to ask the tearoom for some goodies,' he confessed. 'Supporting local industry and all that.'

'Nothing to do with the fact that you don't want to cook,' she teased.

'I love cooking—I'm good at it,' he reminded her archly. 'I just don't do cakes. King Alfred and I have a lot in common. Talking of which, how's Harry's burn?'

'Fine. I took the aloe vera off this morning, and it looks perfectly all right—there's a little red line, but it's not sore. You ought to have a plant.'

'There are all sorts of things I ought to have,' he

said, and she didn't know if she'd imagined it or if there had been a trace of sadness in his voice.

Poor Max. It was all so simple, and he just couldn't see it.

'I'll give you a rooted bit,' she promised. 'Now, getting back to Sunday—do you want me to make a cake, or cut some sandwiches or something? It mustn't look too staged or Harry will smell a rat.'

'He will?'

'He's four, not stupid,' Anna reminded him. 'People he knows don't have big teas unless it's for a birthday party or Grannie and Grandad at Christmas.'

'I concede to your superior knowledge,' he said with a grin. 'I'll buy a cake—unless you can make one of those wicked chocolate ones they sell in there? But we can make sandwiches. Can you get hold of some of that wild boar ham we had in the pub?'

She wrinkled her nose. 'I can, but Harry won't eat it. He only likes egg and cress or banana sandwiches.'

'In which case we'd better have a variety,' Max said, pulling a face. 'I haven't had a banana sandwich for at least twenty-five years.'

'You should,' she said with a laugh. 'They're lovely.'

'Yuck.' He swirled his coffee. 'Do you know Valerie Hawkshead, by the way?'

'Valerie—yes, I do. She and her husband own the fruit shop. Why, has she been in to see you?'

He nodded. He looked concerned, and she wondered what was wrong.

'Problems?' she prompted.

He let out a sigh. 'She came in with headaches and forgetfulness. I sent her to a neurologist, and he said she had depression with retardation. Then she had a fit, and I sent her in again yesterday for a scan. Her husband's just phoned to say they found a brain tumour of some sort, and they've removed it.'

He put his mug down. 'I knew it was more than just depression or premature dementia. That's why I referred her. I can't believe they sent her back on antidepressants without doing a thorough screen.'

'Will she be all right?' Anna asked, concerned for the woman she knew only slightly but who had always been pleasant and friendly.

Max shrugged. 'I don't know. It's too early to say if there's any permanent damage done, and I probably won't be here long enough to find out. That's the trouble with locum work. No continuity.'

He sounded disheartened by that, but again Anna didn't comment. She didn't want to patronise him with platitudes about the patients missing him, or insult his intelligence by telling him that Suzanna was perfectly well qualified. He knew that. She just left the seed of discontent growing quietly in a corner of his mind, and took heart from another ally in her fight against his stubbornness.

Sunday was gorgeous. It wasn't too hot, but Max had mowed the lawn with the little push-mower he'd found in the garage, and had tidied up the rose bed a little so the bushes actually had a chance to be seen. He didn't get as much done as he'd have liked, but he'd cleaned the kitchen and generally made the place look a little better, and Anna brought some flowers from her garden for the mantelpiece in the sitting room.

Harry was playing in the garden, dressed in soft, stretchy shorts and a matching T-shirt, and he looked taller.

Ridiculous, Max told himself. It's only been four weeks. How can he have grown?

He stood at the kitchen window, poised in the act of rinsing the cress for the egg sandwiches, and Anna turned off the cold tap and stood beside him.

'He's grown,' he said, and his voice sounded rough and unused.

Anna gave him an odd look. 'Has he? I hadn't noticed.'

'I think so.'

She looked out again, her face softening.

'You really love him, don't you?' Max said, and he felt a pang of...not envy, exactly, but something akin to it. It must be wonderful to have such a relationship with your child.

He turned the tap on again, washing the cress with great vigour and very little skill, and Anna turned the tap off again and took it out of his hands.

'You're supposed to be rinsing it, not mashing it under the tap,' she scolded affectionately. 'I'll do this. You go outside and spend some time with him.'

He threw her a grateful glance and went out to the garden. 'How are you doing, sport?' he asked.

'OK,' Harry said, chasing a grasshopper across the rough lawn. 'Look, it can jump ever such a long way!'

Max sat down beside him, watching the grasshopper out of the corner of his eye, most of his attention on his son.

Son.

The very word was a miracle, never mind the child. He wanted to reach out and hug him, just to prove he was real and not a figment of his imagination. Instead, he found excuses to touch him—lifting him into a tree, helping him down again, turning him round to show him something—almost anything, just to assuage the terrible urge to sweep him into his arms and crush him against his chest.

'I'm just going to see how your mother's getting on with the sandwiches,' he said, and stood up, almost running into the house in his haste to get away before he made a fool of himself.

Anna met him in the hall, her arms coming out to hug him, and he hugged her back and gave himself time to settle.

'All right now?' she asked gently, and he nodded.

'Yes. Don't know what came over me.'

'Love, I would imagine,' she said matter-of-factly. 'It can get you like that.'

She dropped her arms and went back to the sandwiches, and he went into the sitting room, doing a last scan round to make sure it was tidy. Out of the front window he saw his father's car pull up on the drive, and he went back to the kitchen.

'They're here,' he said, and she turned towards him and looked at him searchingly.

'Are you all right?'

He nodded. 'I'm fine. A bit worried they'll say something. How about you?'

She gave a tight smile, and he realised she was nervous. 'I'll live,' she said, and he gave her a quick hug.

'They'll love you,' he promised, and went to open the door.

'Where is he?' his mother whispered.

'In the garden. You can see him from the window. It's a bit of a shock, he's just like Thomas. Come on in and meet Anna.'

He led them through to the kitchen, and they found

Anna standing nervously by the sink, her eyes alert, her body quiet.

'Anna, I want you to meet my parents, Henry and Clare. Mum, Dad, this is Anna,' he said, and he suddenly found his heart racing. He wanted them to get on, he realised. *Needed* them to get on. He felt suddenly sick with apprehension, but then Anna smiled and held out her hand, and his mother was moving towards her and wrapping her in a motherly embrace, and he knew it was going to be all right.

They were lovely—Max's father just like him but older, with kindly crinkles around eyes that saw right through that outer shell to the things that really mattered, his mother warm and loving and utterly devoted to her stubborn and courageous son.

Her eyes strayed to the window, and Anna moved back, giving them both a better view.

Clare Carter gasped, the hand covering her mouth trembling with reaction. 'Oh, my goodness, he is so like Thomas! I wouldn't have believed it!' Tears filled her eyes, and Anna could see the yearning in her face.

Henry's, too. He stood beside his wife, one hand comfortingly on her shoulder, and together they stared at the grandson they had thought never to have.

'Oh, Max,' his mother said unsteadily, and Anna slipped out, going down the garden to keep an eye on Harry while they stood and watched him from the window and wrestled their emotions into order again.

'Max's mother and father have dropped in—they're going to stay for tea. Isn't that nice?' she told him.

He didn't even look up. 'Yeah. Have we got 'nough?'

'Should have. What are you doing?'

'I found a whole lot of wood lices. They curl up in your hand—look!'

'No, thanks,' she said, suppressing a shudder and looking away. 'Anyway, they're called lice, not lices.'

'This one's really friendly. Hold it!'

'No!'

He chased her with it, down the garden and back again, giggling and squealing with delight, and finally trapped her against the back fence and held out his empty hands.

'Ha-ha!' he said gleefully. 'No wood lices!'

'Lice,' she corrected automatically. 'You are a horrid tease and it's not fair to the wood lice to run around with them. They'll lose their families and be frightened. Where did you drop it?'

'I put him down—I didn't really have him. I just made you run away.'

She hugged him. 'You are a little beast,' she said affectionately.

'Having fun?' Max asked.

Harry broke away from her and ran to his father, talking a mile a minute. Then he skidded to a halt and looked up. 'Is this your mum and dad?' he asked.

Anna watched Max, detecting tiny signs of strain around his eyes as he squatted down next to Harry. 'Yes. They've dropped in on their way past—they've been out for the day, and they're going to stay for tea.'

'Mummy said. Hello.' He tipped his head on one side and looked up at them thoughtfully. 'You look like Max,' he said to Henry Carter.

'That's because I'm his father. Sons often look like their fathers,' he told the boy. How true, Anna thought, looking from Harry to Max, and then Harry lobbed a bomb into the conversation.

'I don't have a father,' he told them matter-of-factly. 'He had to go away.'

There was an awkward silence when all of them seemed to be holding their breath, then Harry went on, 'I've got a granddad, though. I 'spect that counts. He's called George. What's your name?'

'Henry.'

Harry's eyes widened. 'I'm Henry, too! 'Cept everyone calls me Harry, but my proper name's Henry. It's short for Harry.'

'Actually, I think it's the other way round,' Max said, breaking the silence.

'Oh. Never mind. Do you like wood lices?' he asked Clare hopefully.

'Not especially, but your—Max does.'

'Especially down the neck,' he murmured under his breath, and Anna chuckled softly.

So far, so good, she thought.

'I'm hungry,' Harry said, relieving them all of the burden of enduring any more of his entomological exploits. Anna had visions of his victimised woodlice, like tiny armadillos, scuttling for cover in relief.

'Shall we go in for tea?' Max suggested.

'Good idea. No insects,' his mother said with a smile.

'I wouldn't bank on it. This is the country.'

They retired to the relative safety of the sitting room, and Anna helped Max carry in the food while his parents sat down in the comfy chairs and were entertained by their grandson.

'Banana sandwiches—my favourite,' Henry said, tucking in.

'Mine, too,' Harry mumbled.

'Don't talk with your mouth full,' Anna corrected

automatically. 'Anyway, I thought egg and cress were your favourites?'

'Not any more,' he said, siding firmly with his new friend. 'Me 'n Henry like banana best.'

'Dr Carter,' Anna corrected sternly. 'You can't call him Henry, it's not respectful.'

Harry ducked his head. 'Sorry,' he mumbled, and Henry's hand came out and tousled his hair.

'Don't worry about it, son. You call me whatever you want.'

So long as it's Granddad, Anna thought sadly, and met his eyes. They shared a smile of understanding, an understanding shared by his wife.

Anna went out to the kitchen to refill the kettle for more tea, and Clare Carter joined her and gave her a silent hug.

'He's lovely. Such a nice boy. You've done wonders, bringing him up on your own.'

She smiled wryly. 'I've had a lot of help—my parents have been wonderful, and I've got a super neighbour and very good child-care facilities for some of the time.'

Clare hesitated for a moment. 'If you didn't have to work, would you still want to?' she asked cautiously. 'Because, if it's a question of money, we'd be only too happy to help you. I know Max is being obstinate, but I want you to know we're on your side—'

'What are you girls plotting?' Max asked, coming into the kitchen and sliding his arms round his mother's waist.

'We're just talking about how stubborn you are,' she said bluntly. 'And what a tribute Harry is to Anna.'

Anna coloured. 'You're very kind. He's an easy child.'

'His father was,' Clare said, very quietly. 'It's a family thing. Happy genes or something.'

Happy genes, Anna thought. Max's happy genes were a bit overstretched at the moment. If only he'd give in and let himself have everything that was there, waiting for him on a plate—her love, their son's love, the welcome of her family. So much waste.

She shrugged off the sombre thoughts and smiled. 'They'll think they've been abandoned,' she said, topping up the teapot. 'Shall we go back before they finish all the chocolate cake?'

'Thank you.'

Anna smiled sadly. 'My pleasure. It was little enough to do for them,' she told him. 'Fancy a glass of wine?'

'I fancy a hug.'

'You can have both.'

He grinned. 'Sounds good. I left my car at home anyway, so I can walk back.'

They took their wine into her little sitting room and settled down on the sofa, his arm round her shoulders, snuggled up close. 'This is so nice,' he murmured wistfully. 'Harry asleep upstairs, sitting down here with you—all we need now is the cat.'

Right on cue Felix strolled in, leapt onto Max's lap and settled down, kneading his leg with his claws and dribbling furiously.

'You are disgusting,' Anna said affectionately.

'He's just a cat. Ouch! Not that hard.' He peeled the claws out of his skin, tucked the cat's paws under his chest and tickled his ears. It did nothing for the dribbling, but at least that didn't hurt, and his jeans were destined for the wash anyway. He dropped his head back and sighed.

Life was good. This time with Anna and Harry was building him up, filling his memory banks with so much that was infinitely precious. And for a while, at least, he could forget about the future and just pretend...

Anna didn't have the heart to wake him. Anyway, she didn't want to. She sat there, enjoying the cosy moment, until the night grew dark and she thought Max's neck would suffer from being at such a crazy angle.

She eased out from under his arm and lowered it carefully to his side, then propped his head up on a cushion. He sighed and snuggled into it, and she left him there and went and made them coffee.

It was almost midnight, and he needed to go home to bed. He was looking tired—a hangover from the treatment? Possibly. His check-up appointment was the following week, and she was beginning to feel anxious about it.

Not consciously, but inside her there was a deep coil of tension winding slowly but surely tighter. She wondered if she'd have enough adrenaline to cope with it, or if she'd run out or collapse before the check-up.

And how did Max feel? Scared? Resigned?

'Mreouw!'

She looked down at her feet, to see Felix rubbing against her legs, staring hopefully up at her and pleading prettily.

'Cupboard lover,' she told him. 'No. You've been fed. You're fat. Go outside and catch something if you're hungry—work off some calories.'

He was either deaf or eternally hopeful. Whatever,

she nearly fell over him on the way back to the sitting room because he kept trying to block her path, running ahead and sitting down and squawking.

'Oh, cat, shut up,' she said firmly. 'Go away.'

'Who, me?'

Anna laughed. 'No, the cat. I was just going to wake you up—I've made coffee.'

'Wonderful. I love you. I'm as dry as a crisp.'

He levered himself up a bit on the sofa, and she handed him his mug and curled up at the other end, her toes tucked under his thigh. He dropped a hand over her ankles and stroked them absently with his thumb while he sipped his coffee.

'Ah, that's better,' he sighed, dropping his head back against the cushion. 'Your sofa's too comfortable.'

'You're tired.'

He nodded. 'I know. It's the treatment. It takes the stuffing out of you. Anyway, I'm getting older. I'm thirty-four shortly.'

'Poor old man,' she crooned with mock sympathy.

'You don't have to take the mick,' he said archly. 'I know I'm older than you.'

'Not much. I'm thirty now.'

He looked at her strangely. 'I suppose you must be. I still think of you as that young woman of twenty-five that I fell in love with all those years ago. It's as if you've been suspended in time. Whenever I've thought about you, I've tried to imagine you run to seed with lots of grubby, runny-nosed children. Instead, I find you more beautiful than ever, with only one child, and I may be biased but I think he's the most wonderful child in the world.'

She found a wobbly smile. 'Perhaps slightly biased.

I think I might be, too, because I agree. About Harry, anyway. Not about me. I've got squashy and unfit.'

'You're hardly squashy,' he protested. 'Just… womanly.' His eyes darkened, and he groaned. 'Can we change the subject? Thinking about your womanly charms is killing me. I don't suppose we could sneak up to bed?'

'Not unless you're prepared to explain yourself to your son,' she said seriously.

He gave a wry, humourless laugh. 'It was just a thought.' He drained his coffee and stood up. 'Time to go. A brisk walk in the dark might settle my libido down a little.'

'Do you want a torch?'

'Might be an idea. There's no moon tonight. I'd hate to get lost and end up in the ditch with the local drunk.'

'Old Fred? He'll be tucked up in bed at his sister's by now. She keeps him on a fairly tight rein, but not quite tight enough, unfortunately.' She went out to the kitchen, followed by the cat, ever hopeful, and retrieved the torch for Max.

'Here. I think it's all right. It might not be wonderful. Take care.'

He kissed her, a long, slow, lingering kiss that did nothing to settle either his libido or hers, and then opened the door.

The cat, clearly deciding they were too boring for words, hopped out and darted across the road, just as a car shot down the lane.

There was a bump and a howl of pain, and Anna felt her blood run cold.

'Oh, my God,' she whispered, and ran to the edge of the road. 'Felix? Felix, come here. Where are you, boy?'

'Over there,' Max said quietly, shining the torch. 'He's badly hurt. Have you got a board or a stiff mat we can slid him onto?'

'Doormat?' she suggested, picking it up and shaking the loose dirt off it. 'I'll put something on it,' she said shakily, and yanked a pillowcase off the top of the laundry basket at the bottom of the stairs.

She followed Max over the road and found him hunched over Felix, stroking him gently and talking to him in quiet, soothing tones.

'Let's get him inside into the light,' Max suggested. 'We're all a little vulnerable here if there are any more lunatics like that about.'

He took Felix by the scruff and drew him gently onto the covered mat, then lifted him. The cat cried softly in protest, but otherwise lay motionless, panting and gasping.

'Oh, poor baby,' Anna murmured, stroking his head with trembling fingers. 'Oh, Max, what are we going to do?'

'Take him to the vet. Could your parents come and sit with Harry?'

'You could stay. I'll take him.'

Max shook his head. 'No. It's too hard to do that alone. You don't know how badly injured he is. Where is the vet?'

'Ten minutes down the road. I'll ring.'

They'd set the cat down on the sofa, and it was obvious from the strange angle of the limb that one back leg was broken. His face looked battered as well, and Anna bit her lip. Was his jaw broken? The last thing she needed at the moment was a stupendous vet bill.

She rang the vet, filled him in and arranged to meet him, then rang her parents. Her father was out of the door before she'd put the phone down, and arrived as they were loading the cat into her car.

'Don't worry about the boy,' he said, hugging her. 'Hello, Max. Going with her?'

He nodded, and her father said, 'Good man.' He watched them pull away before going inside.

Anna held the cat on her lap on the mat. Her carrier was broken, and she'd kept meaning to get another. Maybe if he came home... 'Turn left—there it is.'

The vet was waiting for them, and met them at the car, lifting Felix gently by the scruff and under the chest and carrying him through to the surgery.

'I'll have to anaesthetise him and X-ray him to make sure his chest isn't compromised,' he said. 'That leg's definitely gone, and possibly his jaw. When did he last eat?'

Anna for once didn't have to feel guilty. 'Hours ago. He was nagging.'

'Good. Right, if you could sign the consent form, I'll do it now, and then you'll know, if you want to hang on.'

She stopped him. 'Is it—? Will the cat recover? Would it be kinder to put him down?'

The vet pulled a face. 'Hard to tell without the X-rays. We need to see what's wrong, but if it's just the leg he should be all right. If it's his pelvis, his bladder and bowel nerves could be affected. We'll have to wait and see.'

'Do whatever's necessary,' Max interrupted. 'If you think it's fair to the cat, do whatever you have to do. I'll pay for it.'

'Max, you can't!' she protested.

'I can. I opened the door.'

'But it's not your fault—'

'Could you please sign the consent form for the X-rays? You can decide who pays for what once we know if he's going to make it, but I'd like to knock him out. He's in a lot of pain.'

Anna signed, her hand trembling, and then looked up. 'Can we come with you and watch?'

'Sure you want to?'

Anna nodded. 'I'm a nurse, he's a doctor. We won't faint or get in the way.'

The vet smiled. 'Come on, then. You can look at the X-rays and see what he's done.'

He clipped a little fur off Felix's foreleg, injected him with anaesthetic and the cat subsided into sleep. 'Right, let's arrange him for these pictures.'

He positioned the body, laid long tubes like sand-bags over his limbs to hold them steady and exposed the plates.

Once they were developed and he was sure they showed everything he wanted to see, he put the cat in a cage on soft synthetic bedding, gave him water for when he woke up and showed them the plates.

'Right. Well, for a start he's going to be a compromised cat, but it could have been worse. The head's all right—bottom jaw's a bit mangled, but I gave it a good wiggle and it's not dislocated or broken, just sore. He's shattered an eye-tooth, lost a chunk of skin under his chin but otherwise his head's fine.

'The chest is good, which is a relief. Sometimes they rupture their diaphragms and the abdominal contents push up into the chest cavity and crush the lungs and heart, which isn't good. They usually sit up then and pant, which he wasn't doing, so I didn't think it was a problem.

'Now, this leg, though.' He shook his head. 'He's

taken the head right off his femur—snapped it clean off the femoral neck. The problems will arise because the end of the femur may have damaged the bladder nerves, so before I operate I want him to pee. Once he's done that, we'll know it's all right to go ahead. If he doesn't, I'm afraid that's it. He's a dead cat.'

'If he does,' Anna said, feeling sicker and more unhappy by the minute, 'if he pees, then what?'

'Then we have to remove the head of the femur—an excision arthoplasty. It's dead now—it's totally severed and lost all its blood supply, so it will start to become necrotic, so we have to remove it. I'll file off the end of the femoral neck, and that will then float in the muscle, build up a layer of callus in the form of cartilage, and create a new joint—a pseudarthrosis.'

Max nodded. 'My uncle has a pseudarthrosis. He had a hip replacement and it went wrong, and they took it away and left him to heal. It's better now than it's been for years, certainly better than the other one. He just wears a built-up shoe.'

'Which the cat, of course, can't do, so he's going to be walking with a limp, but it's quite a common injury, quite a common procedure for us to carry out, and the prognosis is good.'

'If he pees,' Anna said flatly.

'If he pees,' the vet agreed. 'It may be some time. I've given him a painkiller in there with the anaesthetic, so when he comes round he'll be groggy for a while and then might feel like staggering to the litter tray.'

'Ring me,' she pleaded. 'Ring me when he pees. Any time. At home, in the surgery—whatever. Get a message to me, please.'

The vet nodded. 'I think it's hopeful he will. His

pelvis isn't damaged but, of course, the hip joint is part of the pelvis and it's all very close to the nerves. If the swelling spreads, that may cause a problem, but don't worry, I'll ring you the second he's in that litter tray.'

She struggled for a smile. 'Thank you.'

Max thanked the vet as well, then dropped an arm round her shoulders and led her out to the car. Without asking, he put her in the passenger seat and drove her home, and spent the night there in the spare room.

She was glad to have him close. It wasn't close enough, but it was better than in his cottage down the road. She even slept a little, dozing for a few minutes at a time. The night dragged, and only common decency prevented her from ringing the vet and getting him out of bed to check the cat.

At a quarter to seven the phone rang, and she threw herself down the stairs and grabbed the receiver.

'Hello?' she said breathlessly.

'Panic over. He's managed to use his litter tray.'

Relief surged through her. 'Thank you. So what now?'

'Now I go ahead and operate. He'll be here until tomorrow. I want to keep an eye on him and make sure he's all right—make sure all his functions are up to scratch and he's comfortable, and then he'll have to be on cage rest for weeks, I'm afraid.'

'That's fine,' she said weakly. 'I don't mind.'

'I expect he will, though. He'll probably drive you mad, but he can come out for cuddles on your lap. He just mustn't jump up and down on the furniture and, of course, he can't go out until he's properly healed. Anyway, ring up later if you like and see how he got on. I'm sure he'll be fine now.'

'OK. Thank you.'

She put the phone down, shaking with reaction, and found Max's arms round her.

'He peed,' she said. 'He's going to operate this morning.' And promptly howled her eyes out.

CHAPTER EIGHT

FELIX looked incredibly sorry for himself. His leg was shaved at the top, over the hip joint, and there was a line of sutures which Anna hoped he would have the good sense to leave alone, his head was battered and sore, and he was delighted to see them all.

Anna was just delighted that he was alive, and Max insisted on paying the bill. She didn't argue. It came to over a hundred pounds, money she didn't have just lying about, and she vowed to take out pet insurance.

He had to be on cage rest for ages, and for the first few days he was quite good. Because she was out at work all day, she got up early and cuddled him on the bed until she had to get ready, and then again in the evening she had him on her lap in the sitting room, but he was restless and kept trying to jump down, and that was the last thing he was allowed to do until he'd healed.

Harry was wonderfully gentle with him, but she wouldn't let him hold him at first, because she was worried that if Harry prodded a sore bit by accident Felix would scratch or bite him in self-defence. Either that or he'd jump down and hurt himself.

In the end, though, she relented, and he seemed totally content on the little boy's lap and lay there for hours at a time.

It meant she couldn't go out, of course, and so Max did her shopping, Max sat with them in the evenings and, after Harry was in bed and the cat was returned to his borrowed cage, each night Max would systematically drive her up the wall with his goodnight kisses.

Then came the day when Max had to go to London for his check-up.

'When will you know?' she asked him anxiously.

He didn't pretend not to understand. 'A few days,' he said tautly. 'They do the scan, check the blood, run a few tests and let me know. I have to go back for the results.'

She nodded. 'Good luck,' she murmured.

'Thanks.'

She hugged him, unable to help herself, and he hugged her back, his arms tightening so hard he nearly cracked her ribs. 'I love you,' she whispered.

His grip tightened again, just fractionally, and then he let her go. 'I'll be back later. I don't suppose you'd like to get a sitter for the cat and Harry for a few hours and play hooky?'

'I'd love to.' She tried for a smile, but it wouldn't come. She was too tense, too scared, and as the day wore on it grew worse.

It was silly. She kept telling herself it was silly, because he wouldn't get the results today, but it was the fact that the scan would be done and the blood tests taken, and that the whole train would be set in motion.

Without the check-up, without the reminder, they had been able to play at being an ordinary couple and carry on as if nothing had happened.

Was this what it was like for Max always? A long time of forgetting, of putting it out of his mind and ignoring it, and then the harsh reality slamming back?

The sword of Damocles, he'd said, suspended over him on a frayed thread.

She swallowed her fear and tried to concentrate on her patients, but it was difficult. She struggled through her morning surgery, and was just finishing and planning a drive home and a cuddle with her wretched cat when Fred came in.

He'd fallen down, as drunk as a skunk, and been brought in by the local policeman.

'Oh, Fred,' Anna said with a sigh. 'You've cut your head open.'

'Bloody kerb come up and hit me,' he slurred.

'So I see,' she said drily, and smiled at the policeman, another familiar face. 'Stick him there. I'll clean him up and put a stitch in it. Would you like to stay and keep an eye on him? He'll do me for assault, for sure. If you're here, he won't be able to get so exercised.'

The policeman laughed. 'You'll be a good old boy, won't you, Fred?' the young man said, pushing him into a chair in her treatment room and keeping him occupied while she cleaned up the blood down his face and assessed the wound.

'You're going to have a scar, Fred,' she warned, studying the jagged tear. 'Still, we'll soon have you stitched up.'

'Want the doc,' Fred slurred aggressively. 'Not a bloody woman.'

'Fred, shut it, eh?' the policeman said with some affection. 'She's a damn sight prettier than the doctor. Just think yourself lucky. She's younger, too—I expect her eyesight's better. You ought to know when you're well off, mate.'

Anna stifled a smile and swiped Fred's forehead with a spirit wipe. 'Hold still now, this might sting a little.'

'Ow, hell, get her off me!' he yelled, flailing his arms. She whipped the needle out and straightened up.

'Are you going to sit still, or are you going to lie on the bed and I'll tie you down? Which is it to be, Fred? Or you can just go home with your brain hanging out. You never know your luck, some sense might leak in there.'

'Cheeky cow,' he grumbled, but he sat, and she injected him again, putting up with the volley of abuse and invective.

'That's better,' she said comfortingly. 'Now we'll give it a minute to go to sleep, and then I'll sew it together and you'll be good as new.'

Not quite, she thought, standing back some minutes later and studying her handiwork, but better than she'd feared from the state of the cut. At least it had been clean, just a simple split rather than a dirty graze. She didn't fancy her chances of taking a wire brush to his head in this lifetime!

She glanced at her watch as they left, and sighed. She wouldn't get home to Felix, and it seemed unfair to leave him all alone. Now that he wasn't hurting so much, he was bored out of his mind.

She had an idea, and rang her mother. 'Mum, would you mind having Felix in the kitchen in his cage? He could lie there and watch the other cats and the dogs come and go, and Harry could play with him after school, and it would be so much nicer for him.'

'Sounds fine,' her mother agreed. 'I'll get your father to go round with the car and pick him up now, shall I?'

'You're a star,' Anna said, and then hesitated. 'I don't suppose you want Harry for the night as well, do you? Max has been to London for a check-up and tests. I'd just like to spend some time with him tonight.'

'Of course,' her mother said without hesitation. 'He's got plenty of things here. Don't worry about it—and I'll take him to school in the morning if you like. Then you don't have to worry about getting up so early.'

She could feel her colour rising, but fortunately her mother couldn't see it. 'Lovely. Thanks, Mum. I owe you.'

'You owe me nothing,' her mother said gently. 'Just be happy.'

Anna cradled the phone and bit her lip. She'd love to be happy. All she wanted was the chance...

The train journey was interminable, from the hot, over-crowded confusion of the tube to the mercifully air-conditioned but still overcrowded chaos of the mainline service to Ipswich. Max crossed the road, went over the bridge and down to the car park, retrieved his car and headed for Wenham Market. It took half an hour, and without thinking he pulled up outside Anna's house, locked the car and walked up the path.

The door swung open before he had time to touch the bell, and he stepped through the open doorway, kicked the door shut behind him and engulfed her in his arms.

'God, I hate London,' he mumbled into her hair, and kissed her jaw, her cheek, her nose, her eyelids—and then her mouth, settling on those soft, warm, eager lips with a sigh of homecoming.

Reluctantly he drew away, dredging up a lopsided smile. 'We can't,' he groaned. 'Harry.'

'Harry's at Mum's. So's the cat. So, my place or yours?'

He thought of his car, parked outside her house in broad daylight for all to see, and thought of the secluded intimacy of his cottage down its quiet lane.

'Mine? It's more private. I want to be alone with you, without people dropping in or wondering what I'm doing here.'

She nodded. 'Can I stay over?'

He grinned lazily. 'Just try leaving.'

She chuckled. 'Give me a minute to grab some things. I can bring my uniform and then I don't have to come home. Hang on.'

She ran upstairs, her legs flying, and he watched her bottom vanish round the corner with regret. She had a pretty bottom, rounded and soft, without being big— like her breasts. A groan rose in his throat, and he closed his eyes and waited impatiently. He needed two things. A drink was the second. Anna, without doubt, was the first.

He went into the kitchen, drank a glass of water from the tap and was back at the bottom of the stairs as she came down, bag in hand. They all but ran down the path, jumped into his car and didn't quite exceed the speed limit going out to his cottage.

They didn't make it upstairs for a while. Instead, they closed the front door and reached for each other, tearing off their clothes with trembling hands, their eyes fevered, and he lifted her against him and drove into her with a groan of relief. Her legs coiled round him, her mouth sought his and he propped her against the door and plunged into her again and again, until with a shuddering cry she collapsed sobbing in his arms.

His body stiffened, he dropped his head against her shoulder and locked his knees, and when the tremors had passed, he lowered her feet to the floor and kissed her again.

'I love you,' he said raggedly. 'It's been so long.'

'Only a week.'

He gave a strangled laugh. 'Is that all? It feels like months. It's the tension.' He eased away from her and smiled wryly. 'I'm sorry. That wasn't very dignified.'

'I don't care.' Her hand came up and cupped his cheek, her thumb stroking the side of his mouth, dragging the damp skin. 'I love you, too. I've missed you today. It's been such a long day without you.'

Her eyes sparkled, and she blinked and turned away, gathering their clothes in a heap in her arms.

'Let's go to bed,' he suggested softly, and she nodded and went upstairs. He followed her, watching the soft globes of her buttocks tense with every step, and wanted her again. Still. For ever.

He backed away from that thought. Just tonight, he promised himself. Just think about tonight. Don't look ahead. Deal with today. Love her tonight as if it's the last time.

He took the clothes out of her hands and dropped them on a chair, then drew her back into his arms. 'Where were we?' he murmured.

Her arms slid round him and she eased closer, her eyes widening with surprise as she felt his response.

'We were in the hall, up against the front door like alley cats,' she said with a smile. 'Now we're in your bedroom. Shall we take advantage of that nice big bed?'

'What a good idea. I couldn't have had a better one myself.'

He flicked back the quilt, groaned as he watched her slide under the covers, her nipples sassy and pert and asking for attention, and followed her in, drawing her into his arms.

'This time I'm going slow,' he promised.

'Don't change anything on my account,' she said with a laugh, and he groaned and moved over her.

Forget the foreplay, he thought. They didn't need it. They were both wound up so tight they were about to explode, and as he entered her she shuddered and sobbed. He felt her body convulsing round him, her hands raking his back, her mouth hot and eager against his throat, and he abandoned all attempts at finesse and let nature drive him.

It should have been quieter, more gentle, their appetites slaked a little by the first time.

It wasn't. It was, if anything, more devastating, more powerful, more intense than ever before, and as he lay in her arms, unable to move, stunned by the awesome beauty of their loving, he wondered if he would ever find the strength to leave her.

Because he'd promised himself that if by a hideous twist of fate he was no longer in remission then he would go.

It all hung on the results, and the wait was going to be harder than anything he'd had to endure before, because this time there was so much more at stake.

Don't think about it, he told himself. Just enjoy her. Give her what you can. Wait.

Be patient.

And pray...

'Anna?'

'Yes? Is that Mrs Carter?'

'It is. Anna, I hope you don't mind me phoning—I got your number from directory enquiries. It's about Max.'

Her heart crashed against her ribs. 'What about him?' she asked tensely.

'Nothing bad! Don't worry. It's his birthday on Sunday, but I expect you know that.'

'No, I didn't. He's failed to share it with me,' she said drily.

His mother laughed. 'Oh, well, that sounds like Max. Anyway, he's coming for lunch. I thought I'd ask him to bring you, and he doesn't know it but I've asked the others—Andrew and Frankie and Joel and their other halves, and the children. It'll be a bit chaotic, and I don't know how you feel about it, but I wondered... would you mind bringing Harry?'

Warmth flooded her, the warmth of his family reaching out to her, including her and her son—Max's son, of course, and maybe she was only included as an appendage, but Mrs Carter had seemed genuinely pleased to meet her.

'I'd love to come and bring Harry. The only thing is, you won't say anything, will you? Not to the children. If Max's brothers and sister know, I think that's a good idea, but, please, make sure nobody lets it out. If we decide to tell Harry, I do want it to be a considered decision and not just a blunder.'

Mrs Carter hastened to reassure her. 'Of course. Don't worry, I'll prime them all. Are you going to come with him in the car, or on your own?'

'With him, I think,' she said thoughtfully. 'Otherwise he'll smell a rat. If he doesn't know about the others, he'll just think it's a birthday lunch and we've been invited.' Something else occurred to her. 'Would you like to ask him to invite me, and we'll pretend we've never had this conversation? Then he won't be suspicious.'

Mrs Carter laughed delightedly. 'Oh, Anna, what a good idea. I'll ring him now.'

'Before you go,' Anna said quickly, 'I don't suppose you've got any ideas about what I could give him?'

There was a long silence. 'Nothing lasting—nothing built to endure for generations,' she said finally, her voice tinged with sadness. 'He's got this thing about it. Feels he's not going to be here for long so there's no point. I usually give him clothes or something like that, which he has to have regardless, and make a fuss of him.'

How incredibly sad and defeatist, Anna thought, and wondered what on earth she could give him.

Then it came to her. Flowers. Nobody ever gave men flowers, and yet when her father had been ill once and her mother had given him flowers, he'd been delighted.

Yes. She'd give him flowers, and she'd arrange them herself. A big basket of them to stand on top of the wood-burning stove in his cottage, and look gorgeous. And Harry could draw him a picture.

She went to the florist during her break in the morning and ordered a lined basket, and planned the arrangement. Masses of colour and lots of roses from her mother's garden, with dark green foliage, her favourite combination.

She'd arrange them on Saturday evening—unless Max had plans for the evening, in which case she'd arrange them earlier and hide them in her garden shed. Or, better still, do it at her mother's, where he definitely wouldn't see them. That made sense, as she'd pick the flowers from her mother's wonderful garden on Friday night and condition them in the scullery until she arranged them.

Excellent.

She walked along from the florist to the surgery, and passed Fred lurking near the bus shelter, looking for cigarette ends on the ground. 'Fred?' she said, as she approached, and he jumped guiltily.

'Dear me, Sister, you scared the living daylights out of me—what you trying to do, frighten me to death?'

She suppressed a smile. 'I was expecting you earlier,' she told him. 'You had an appointment to see me this morning to have your stitches out, and you didn't turn up. What happened to you?'

'Oh, the usual,' he said. 'Bad head—it's the arteritis in my neck.'

'You don't have arthritis in your neck,' she told him drily. 'You probably had a hangover.'

'It's my sister's pillows—mean as an old rattlesnake she is, won't buy me a new one.'

'It's a wonder she puts up with you at all, never mind buy you new pillows. Come on, come over to the surgery with me now and I'll take them out for you.'

He mumbled a protest, but she took his arm and guided him across the street, staggering slightly, and propelled him into her room and sat him down. 'Right, this won't take a moment. It's healed quite well, considering.'

'Considering what?' he asked grumpily.

Considering it's bathed in neat alcohol, she nearly said, but then thought better of it. 'Considering it was only a few days ago,' she lied. 'Right, hold still. That's it. Lovely. Off you go, then, and take care.'

'Is that all?' he asked incredulously. 'Could have done that myself with the old cut-throat.'

The idea of him with a cut-throat razor left her cold with horror. 'Go on, Fred, go home.'

'No. Chip shop opens soon. They give me last night's cold fish—I tell them it's for the dog,' he said, wheezing and cackling at his own craftiness.

'Fred, you don't have a dog,' she said patiently.

'I know—clever, ain't it? And they don't know!'

I bet they do, Anna thought with exasperated affection. 'Go on, Fred, hop it. I've got patients to see.'

He grumbled his way out of the door, and she puffed a little air freshener around the room to disguise the smell a bit, then called her next patient.

She recognised the young woman, but she didn't know where from at first. 'Jenny, isn't it? Come on in and sit down.'

'Thanks. First of all, how's the cat?' she asked, and then the penny dropped.

'He's fine—I thought I recognised you. You work at the vet's, don't you?'

'At the moment—I'm pregnant now, so I won't be doing it too much longer. That's why I'm here—for routine blood tests.'

'Oh, lovely. Congratulations. When's it due?'

The girl snorted softly. 'January—and it's not exactly wonderful news. I'm not married, and he's gone off already.'

Anna prepared her syringes and swabbed the inside of the girl's elbow. 'I've got a little boy. He's four, and his father disappeared very early on in my pregnancy without ever knowing. Believe me, it's possible to have a baby on your own and bring it up and do everything a married parent would do. It's just a lot harder sometimes, but at others it's easier, so it sort of balances. Will you have help?'

She nodded. 'My mum. She lives near me. She's going to help me, because I'll have to go back to work. I couldn't get rid of it, though. It's my baby, isn't it?' she said simply. 'I reckon we're stuck with each other.'

Anna smiled at her. 'Just enjoy it. Babies are wonderful, and they grow up so fast. Every stage is different—some are worse than others, but all of them pass. Just remember that when it's teething or has colic or night terrors or temper tantrums. Everything passes!'

'Including pregnancy, thank goodness,' the girl said with a laugh. 'I've been as sick as a parrot for the first few weeks, but now I feel better.'

'Just one thing,' Anna warned her as she dropped the last sample in the bag, 'wear gloves and wash your hands very thoroughly if you handle any cats or dogs or their dirty litter. You can't risk getting toxoplasmosis during your pregnancy.'

'Right. I'll be careful—I had heard about it, but it's so easy to forget. Thanks.'

Anna called her next patient, and Max stuck his head round the door. 'Can we have lunch?' he asked quickly.

'Sure—what time?'

'When you're finished. I haven't got any calls today.'

She nodded. 'OK. I've got two more patients.'

'Fine. I'll wait.'

He blew her a kiss, and she felt a warm glow surround her that stayed with her after he'd gone. She must have looked different, because both of her patients remarked on how well she looked, and how happy!

She sent the last one off with a new dressing, and went out to find Max. He was in the garden, sitting amongst the roses as usual, and she was suddenly glad she'd decided to give him flowers.

He stood up when she went out and smiled at her. 'Just smell this rose,' he said, and she stuck her nose right into it and sniffed slowly.

'Mmm, gorgeous. It's a Blanc Double de Coubert,' she told him. 'My mother's got some in her garden.'

He looked wistful for a moment, then his mouth tipped in a lopsided smile. 'Lunch?' he suggested.

'Where?'

'I thought we could buy some sandwiches in the shop and walk down to the river. I just wanted some fresh air and space, and I've got something to ask you.'

Sunday? she thought, but said nothing. They went into the shop and bought some sandwiches and a bottle of Max's 'designer' water, and headed down the hill to the river. There was a mill, and they sat on the bank by the millstream and munched their sandwiches, and Anna waited.

'Are you busy on Sunday?' he asked finally, taking the last bite of sandwich.

'No—why?'

He shrugged. 'It's my birthday. My mother always does lunch or something for me. She asked me to ask you and Harry. I think they just want to see him again—she hasn't stopped talking about him.'

I know, she nearly said, and stopped herself in the nick of time. 'That would be lovely,' she said instead. 'What sort of time?'

'Oh, leaving here about eleven, I suppose. We want to be in Cambridge by half past twelve, and I don't want to go like a bat out of hell.'

'OK.'

'And on Saturday night, I thought we'd have our

own private celebration,' he said softly, his meaning clear. 'I thought I might take you out for dinner, then lure you back to my den and have my wicked way with you.'

She smiled. 'You won't have to do much luring,' she assured him.

His mouth tipped in a grin. 'Is that right, you hussy?'

'Absolutely. We have to go, we'll be late. You've got an antenatal clinic and I've got to stand in for the midwife.'

'What about tonight?' he asked, getting to his feet and pulling her up. 'Are you doing anything?'

'Visiting my cat,' she said with a laugh. 'Want to join us?'

'Poor old boy. How is he?'

'Less bored than he would be at home,' she replied. 'He'll live. He's driving Mum mad, I think. We could go for a walk through the woods, if you like. I know you won't finish until about six-thirty, but if you come to the farm for supper, we could take a stroll afterwards. Fancy that?'

'Sounds a bit healthy,' he said with a grin. 'Won't your mother mind?'

'Not at all,' she promised, and made a note to ring her mother and warn her so there would be enough to go round. Not that there was any danger that there wouldn't be. She usually did enough for an army.

'Tell me, any news of Valerie?' she asked as they passed the fruit shop.

'Yes—she's progressing well. Her headaches are better, her mind's much clearer and she's feeling more like herself all the time, apparently. Let's just hope it continues.'

They were just turning into the surgery premises

when a young lad skidded round the corner on his bike, swerved to miss them and skidded on some loose gravel. The bike flew out from under him, he crashed into the wall and for a second they all froze.

A lorry thundered past, galvanising them all into action. Max ran towards him, with Anna in hot pursuit, and the boy started to get up. Blood poured from his mouth, and he started to shake with reaction.

'It's Paul, isn't it?' Anna said. 'Paul Seager?'

He nodded.

'Are you all right?' Max asked calmly. 'Anywhere particular hurt?'

'Mouth,' he mumbled, and then he closed his eyes and started to cry.

'He's shocked—let's take him in,' Max said, and Anna put her arm round his shoulders and steered him towards the door.

'You picked the right place to fall off, anyway, Paul,' she said, trying to distract him.

The receptionist did a mild double-take. 'Good heavens,' she said, 'I thought we were busy enough, without you two going out touting for business!'

Max shot her a grin. 'Just hold all our patients for a few minutes, could you? We want to make sure there's no harm done.'

'Of course,' she agreed.

Anna pushed the door open, led Paul through the waiting room and said to Max, 'Your place or mine?'

One brow arched eloquently, but he managed to keep a straight face. 'Yours. You've got all the equipment.'

She stifled a laugh. They went into her treatment room and laid the young man down on the couch, and

Anna covered him with a blanket while Max washed his hands and snapped on some gloves.

'Right,' he said kindly, 'let's take a look at you, Paul. What have you done to your mouth?'

He opened it carefully, and Max turned back his top lip and found a nasty puncture wound. Two of his teeth were broken, just chipped at the bottom edge, and Max gently but thoroughly checked the wound in his lip to make sure that there were no fragments of teeth left inside.

'Ow,' the boy cried, and Max apologised but carried on. Anna held his hand, and when Max was satisfied she wiped his face, gave him a mouthwash and tidied him up.

'I think your mum's going to have a bit of a fit,' she said, looking at the state of his clothes. His trousers were ripped, his shirt was drenched with blood and he'd dripped on his trainers.

'It's the holidays,' Max said with a grin. 'You'd be safer at school. Right, you need to see the dentist about those teeth, but I don't think you've got an urgent problem. They might be a little bit sensitive to hot and cold for a while, and so will your lip, so be careful to have everything tepid for a bit, OK?'

He nodded.

'Now, anywhere else hurt? Hands, knees, ankles, elbows?'

The boy shook his head. 'My mom'll kill me. These trousers were new.'

'It was an accident,' Anna soothed him. 'Mums only kill when you've been stupid. Trust me, I know.'

'I was being stupid,' Paul said dolefully. 'I was going much too fast. I nearly hit you.'

'Well, if it's any comfort,' Max told him, 'it's a good

job you swerved to avoid us, because if you'd gone straight out into the main road like that, that darned great lorry that came along a moment later would have killed you for sure. Tell your mother that. Is she at home at the moment?'

He nodded, his eyes wide.

'Well, perhaps if you give Anna all the details, she can ring your mother and tell her all about your accident, and she can come down and collect you, all right? And I'll make sure your bike's in out of the road so it doesn't get nicked.'

It held them up, of course. They worked their way through the antenatal clinic together, Anna weighing mums and checking blood pressures and urine samples, Max feeling the lie of the babies and listening to their heartbeats and asking about problems.

She finished after the antenatal, but he still had a surgery to do, so she left him to it and went to see her mother—hopefully in time before she cooked the supper, because in all the chaos with young Paul Seager she'd forgotten to ring about Max joining them.

'No problem,' Sarah said with a smile. 'It'll be nice to have him here. Talk to the cat—it's bored to death.'

So Anna sat on the floor beside the cage and tickled the cat through the bars, and her mother handed her a cup of tea and she told her about the flowers she was planning for Max. 'I hope you've got lots, or shall I go and buy them? I just felt it would be nicer if they came from here.'

'I agree,' her mother said. 'I've got tons, you know that. I always have tons. Just leave me some of the pink stuff for a wedding next week, that's all.'

Anna laughed. 'I won't take that much. I want to be able to carry the darned thing! I thought I'd come and

pick them tomorrow morning early and put them in
cold water till Saturday. He wants to go out for dinner
on Saturday, so I can't do them on Saturday night.'

She had a moment of doubt. 'You don't think he'll
feel I'm being a cheapskate, do you?' she asked worriedly. 'Only his mother said he hates anything that
lasts, because he thinks it'll outlast him, and I couldn't
think of anything else apart from food. Perhaps I
should have just ordered him a hamper from somewhere really smart.'

'And spent hundreds of pounds? Don't be silly,' her
mother told her. 'Anyway, he'll love them. Men never
get flowers, and it's such a shame.'

Thus encouraged, she took Max on a tour of the
flower garden later that evening, and made a mental
note of the flowers he particularly loved, then the following morning she cut them and put them up to their
necks in cold water in the scullery, and on Saturday
she made some excuse about the cat and arranged them
in her big wicker basket.

'Oh, darling, they're lovely,' her mother said, going
all misty-eyed.

'I hope he thinks so. I wonder if I ought to go and
get him something else? Chocolates or something? A
pen to use for work?'

'No. Stop fussing, and go. You'll be late for dinner.'

'Are you sure you're all right to have Harry again?'

Her mother smiled sadly. 'Of course. It's not for
long, after all, is it? Either Max will stay, and you'll
all be together, or…' She trailed off.

'Or he'll go, one way or the other,' Anna finished
softly. 'I know.'

CHAPTER NINE

ANNA heard her father's pickup truck stop outside Max's cottage at seven the next morning. She slipped out of bed without waking him, crept downstairs in his dressing-gown and opened the door.

'Where do you want them?' her father asked.

'On the wood-burner in the sitting room. I'll open the door.'

She led him silently through, and helped him put the flowers down on the black iron stove. They filled the empty wall above, and looked wonderful.

'Clever girl,' her father said, hugging her. 'Wish him a happy birthday from us. Here's a bottle of wine for you to share later.'

He handed her a bottle of bubbly, and she kissed him and closed the door softly behind him.

'Annie?'

She went to the foot of the stairs, the champagne still in her hand. 'Hi. Did I wake you? Sorry. Someone came to the door.'

'Have they gone?'

'Yes.'

He padded downstairs, dressed only in a pair of hastily tugged-on jeans, and stopped dead in the sitting room doorway.

'What's that?' he asked, his face a picture.

'Happy birthday,' she said softly.

He looked at her, stunned. 'Are they for me?'

She nodded.

149

'From you?'

Again, she nodded.

'They're beautiful! Oh, Annie…' His voice cracked, and he dragged her into his arms and hugged her till she thought her ribs would break. 'No one's ever given me flowers before,' he mumbled into her hair, and after a moment he lifted his head.

His eyes were sparkling, his lashes clogged, and he went over to the arrangement and breathed deeply. 'It's got those wonderful roses in it—the ones with the French name—and the gladioli, and the—oh, all sorts!' He turned to her, laughing. 'You took me round the garden and pumped me about these,' he accused, pointing a finger at her chest. 'You crafty little minx.'

'Of course. Women are devious,' she said, thinking of his mother and the surprise party waiting for him. Perhaps she'd better change the subject! She held out the bottle. 'This is from my parents. They said happy birthday.'

He took it and looked at her. 'I'll put it in the fridge, and we can have it later. Just now I want to thank you properly.'

They picked Harry up from her parents at eleven o'clock, and Max thanked them for the wine and for donating the flowers. Her mother had a big kiss, which gave her pink-eye, and her father hugged him and patted him awkwardly on the back.

'Have a nice day,' they said warmly, and Anna strapped Harry into his booster seat in her car and they set off. They were taking her car so that Max could drink, as it was his birthday celebration, and Anna had a feeling the family intended him to celebrate it whether he wanted to or not! It took just over an hour, and by the time they arrived Harry was beginning to fidget.

They turned onto the drive and Max heaved a sigh of relief. 'Thank God for that. I did wonder if the whole darned clan would be here—my mother's not beyond that.'

Anna said nothing. She was too busy biting her lip. She parked the car on the drive, beside one other, and wondered where the other cars were hidden. In the garage, perhaps? It looked big enough, and the car on the drive wasn't arousing his suspicions.

'Whose is that?' she asked, indicating it.

'Oh, Mother's. She always leaves it out. Too lazy to put it away. Come on, let's go and find them. Out you get, Harry.'

He was heading for the side of the house when the front door opened and his father appeared. 'Hello, Max. Happy birthday, son. Anna, Harry, hello. Come on in. You've made good time.'

'Anna's driving. You can blame her if we're early,' he said with a smile, and hugged his father. 'Good to see you again. You look well.'

'You look pretty good yourself. Come on in, let's find your mother.'

She followed them through the door, and Max's father said to him, 'I think she's in the drawing room. Go on in, I just have to do something in the kitchen.'

He held back, and Max opened the door, to find streamers and balloons and all sorts dangling round the room. 'Mother?' he said, bemused, and then people jumped up from behind the furniture. He stood there, totally astonished, a stunned expression on his face.

'Happy birthday!' they all chorused, and he laughed

and hugged them all, one by one. 'Mother, I'll get you,' he threatened, but he didn't sound cross at all.

He turned to Anna. 'Did you know about this?' he asked, and all eyes swivelled to her.

'I confess,' she said with a smile.

He shook his head despairingly, and then he caught sight of Harry and froze.

'By the way, everyone, let me introduce you,' Clare was saying. 'Anna, this is Joel, and his wife Patty, and their children Thomas and Daisy, and this is our daughter Frankie, and her husband Rick, and their children Emily and Stephen—oh, I don't know where they are. Under the table, I think. And this is Andrew, and Julia, and little Sophie. Everybody, this is Anna, a colleague of Max's, and her son, Harry.' She peered round. 'Where is Harry, by the way?'

'Here,' he said, coming out from behind Anna and peering at something in his hand. 'I found a spider. It's dead.' Then he looked up and smiled, totally unaware of the impact he was having, and said, 'Hello.'

There was a collective intake of breath, and all eyes were glued to him. All adult eyes, anyway. The children were too busy playing tag. After a stunned second they pulled themselves together and started talking all at once. Max heaved a sigh of relief and grabbed his mother, dragging her out of the room.

'Do they know?' he asked in an undertone.

'Yes—the adults.'

'I'll kill you if this goes wrong,' he threatened.

'Nothing's going to go wrong,' she promised. 'It's a little party. Just enjoy it.'

Lunch was a splendid affair, a huge sit-down meal for all sixteen of them at a great refectory table which had been somehow carried out to the garden and placed in the shade of a lovely tree. Admittedly they were a bit squashed up, but nobody seemed to mind, and the children were all muddled up amongst them and helped and corrected and encouraged by all the adults regardless.

Harry joined in without hesitation, wedged between Frankie and Joel, and he seemed to be having a wonderful time.

Wine flowed, because nobody was driving for ages. Anna was cautious and restricted herself to one glass of champagne, just in case Max decided they needed to leave suddenly if things got out of hand.

After the meal everyone retired, groaning, to the garden chairs dotted around in the shade, or sat on the grass under the trees on rugs. Some carried on drinking wine, others had tea or coffee. Having made sure Max and Harry were happily engaged, Anna went into the house to see if she could help with the clearing up.

Predictably, the women were in the kitchen, and as she walked in they fell silent. Not surprising, Anna thought. She and Harry were bound to have been the topic of conversation.

'Can I help?' she asked.

Clare handed her a teatowel. 'You could wipe up the crystal—it can't go in the dishwasher. Frankie, darling, put the kettle on. Julia, show Anna where the crystal goes.'

Patty was up to her elbows in suds, and smiled at Anna as she picked up the first glass. 'Nice to meet you, by the way. I didn't get a chance to talk to you at lunch, we were too far apart. You're very brave, agreeing to do this, you know. Clare can be a bit of a bully.'

Clare laughed. 'You exaggerate. I didn't have to bully at all, did I?'

'How can she say yes, Mother?' Frankie said with a smile.

'Actually, she didn't have to bully me,' Anna admitted. 'I wanted to meet you all. I've been telling Max how unfair it is to keep Harry from his family, but he's—'

'Stubborn?' Julia offered. 'Runs in the family, like wooden legs,' she said drily. 'The whole lot of them are tarred with the same brush. Stunning blue eyes and utterly intractable. Talk about mules being difficult.'

'We're wonderful!' Frankie protested, and Patty and Julia laughed.

'In your dreams,' Patty said fondly. 'He's gorgeous, by the way. He's a credit to you.'

Anna followed the direction of her gaze through the kitchen window, and saw Harry playing with the others. It was some kind of organised game, and he was joining in with the others as if he'd always been there. She felt her eyes prickling, and blinked hard.

'Thank you,' she said in a low voice. 'I've always wondered if he had any cousins. I'm an only child, so Max's family were his only hope. I'm so glad he's getting on well with them.'

Clare put her hand on Anna's shoulder. 'Anna, you won't forget where we are, will you? If you and Max should part again, or if anything should happen to him, God forbid, you won't forget we're here, will you? You're part of the family now, you and Harry. With or without Max. I mean that.'

Anna couldn't help the tears. They welled up in her eyes, and she blinked them away and turned into

Clare's arms, hugging her hard. 'Thank you,' she said unsteadily. 'Thank you so much.'

'Oh, Lord, you're going to start us all off,' Frankie said, sniffing. 'Come on, they'll be in here in a minute, demanding tea, and the place is still in chaos.'

Clare released her and went back to sorting her salads and leftovers, Patty handed her another glass, Julia started wiping down the worktops and Frankie, redundant at that moment, went outside and started gathering up abandoned wineglasses.

The chatter became more general, and they included Anna whenever possible, telling her stories about the family, asking her about her life and Harry's childhood and her own parents, until she felt she'd known them all for years.

And she knew that no matter what happened to Max, they'd be there for her, like a loving safety net, supporting and sustaining each other through whatever was to come.

She felt the tension ease out of her, the tightened coil of fear inside shift and relax—not much, but just a little. Enough. All they had to do was get through the next few days until Max got his results, and somehow even that seemed less terrifying now than it had.

A problem shared, and all that.

It was a lovely day.

Clare had said it would be, and she'd been right, of course. It went without a hitch.

Well, almost. There was the spellbinding moment just after the huge birthday cake had been brought out, blazing. Max had blown out the candles quickly before the tree caught fire, and they'd all sung 'Happy

Birthday', and then, in a clear, piping voice, one of the children called Harry Thomas, and everyone froze.

Then Daisy started laughing. 'Emily called Harry Thomas,' she crowed. 'Isn't that funny?'

'But he looks like Thomas,' Emily said petulantly.

There was another pregnant silence, then Frankie said lightly, 'When I was at school there was a girl who looked just like me. We were always getting into trouble for each other's scrapes. I never worked out if we got into half or twice as much trouble. I suspect twice.'

And the conversation picked up seamlessly, and Max started to breathe again. 'That was close,' he said to Anna under his breath. 'I think we need to get out of here before anything else happens.'

She nodded. 'I agree. The kids are all as sharp as tacks. It won't take them five minutes to work it out if Harry tells them his father went away.'

Frankie appeared at Anna's side and hugged her. 'Incidentally, I think you're just the woman for my brother. He looks happier than he's looked for years. Keep up the good work,' she whispered.

'What are you plotting?' Max asked suspiciously.

'She said I'm wearing you out,' Anna lied with a wink. 'Come on, we need to go. We've got a drive and Harry's tired.'

They made their goodbyes and drove slowly home, and Harry fell asleep in the back of the car. It was nearly nine by the time they got home, and she dropped Max off, pausing to give him a lingering kiss.

'Thank you so much for today,' he said softly. 'I'll see you tomorrow. I'm going to go and enjoy my flowers.' He kissed her again. Turning in the seat, he pressed a kiss to his fingers and laid them gently on Harry's brow. 'Goodnight, little one,' he murmured.

Then he was out of the car, closing the door softly behind him and pushing it till it clicked. Anna drove up to her cottage, took Harry up to bed via the bathroom and slipped him under the covers without really waking him.

She phoned her mother to ask after the cat, curled up in a chair with a cup of tea and reflected on the events of the day. It had been a good day—a wonderful day—and she felt surrounded by the love and acceptance of the entire Carter clan.

That they all adored Max was obvious. What was equally obvious was that they were desperate for an opportunity to love Harry in the same way, and she vowed that, whatever Max decided to do, she would keep in touch with his family.

The flowers made the whole house smell wonderful. Max poured himself a glass of juice, put on a CD of choral music and lay back in his chair, feet up, and relaxed.

He missed Annie, but he felt she was here with him, with the flowers she'd chosen and arranged for him. He breathed deeply, inhaled the delicate, intoxicating fragrance and sighed contentedly.

Harry had had fun, he thought with a smile, remembering how he'd joined in with his cousins. He just seemed to fit right in.

It was a sobering thought. Perhaps Annie was right, he admitted reluctantly. Perhaps it was wrong to deny Harry and the rest of them access to each other.

Still, the results would be revealed in a day or two, and he would have a better idea of what to do. If he was still in remission, then perhaps it was time to tell Harry that he was his father. If not…

If not didn't bear thinking about. He'd have to go through another programme of treatment, another gruelling period of waiting to hear, of further tests, of more treatment, more tests…

He'd worry about it if it happened. For now, he'd listen to the music, enjoy the beauty of the flowers and relax…

'You will come back? No matter what they say, you will come back and tell me, won't you?'

Max hugged Annie gently. 'I will come back,' he said, fear coiling in him. He was lying. If his results were bad, he'd decided not to come back. He'd check into a hotel, then find somewhere else to live. He'd never see her again.

He kissed her hungrily, and she hugged him hard, hanging on till the last moment. 'Annie, I have to go,' he said gruffly, and she released him reluctantly.

He slid behind the wheel and shut the car door, his eyes locked with hers. She knows, he realised. She knows I won't come back if it's bad.

He swallowed, gunned the engine and shot off down the road, blinking hard. Dammit, he wouldn't cry. He wouldn't look back. He wouldn't…

He glanced in the mirror and she was just a blur, standing with one arm upraised, the other wrapped tightly round her waist. She went out of focus, and he blinked again and dragged his eyes back to the road. No point killing himself. Not now, at least.

Not ever. He couldn't do it to his parents, even if there were times when the thought had been more than welcome.

He couldn't do it to Anna, or Harry. There was a picture in his wallet of Harry, laughing, in the garden at the cottage. He was beautiful, mischievous and bright-eyed, and the camera had caught his expression exactly.

At the thought of his son, a huge lump blocked his throat and he swallowed hard. 'Stop thinking about him,' he ordered himself, and turned the radio on to a news programme. Maybe it would take his mind off it.

The train journey was as awful as ever, and he crossed London on the tube and arrived with only five minutes to spare. Nevertheless, he had to wait, and every minute was agony. The hands on the clock seemed to crawl, and he was so tense, so overwound, that when the nurse called his name he felt his heart lurch with fear.

Not for himself, but for all he would lose if this went wrong.

Gathering the last shreds of his self-control, he stood up and walked towards his destiny.

It was the longest day of Anna's life. She'd spent the night with Max, making love tenderly until they were too tired to move, and then sleeping, wrapped in each other's arms. He'd taken the early train, and she'd cleared up the house, taken a couple of dead flowers out of the arrangement and then gone to her parents' house.

Harry was almost a permanent resident now, she thought wearily, and decided that, no matter what today revealed, Harry would know that Max was his father, and she would stay with him and marry him if she had to handcuff him to get him to the altar!

They belonged together, no matter what Max said.

'For better, for worse, for richer, for poorer, in sickness and in health, till...'

She stopped there. No. She'd be positive. He was all right. He was going to be all right.

He had to be all right.

She ran upstairs and found her mother coming out of the bathroom.

'Has he gone?' she asked softly, and Anna nodded.

'Yes. He's getting the early train. Is Harry awake yet?'

'No. Why don't you go and have a cuddle with him?'

She did, sliding under the covers in her clothes and snuggling him up against her. He was small and sleepy and warm, and she tucked her nose into the side of his neck and sniffed. He smelt wonderful, her very own little horror, and she loved him more than she could have believed possible.

'Hello, Mummy,' he mumbled, and turned in her arms, cuddling up against her and jabbing his knees in her stomach. She kissed his nose.

'Time to get up, sleepyhead,' she said affectionately. 'What do you want for breakfast?'

'We've got gooses' eggs, Grannie said,' he told her. 'We're going to have them scrambled on toast.'

'I'd better help you get ready, then, hadn't I, because scrambled eggs don't keep? Up you get!'

She threw back the cover and scooped him out, and he sat on her knee and hugged her and gave her a wet but very welcome kiss.

Dear Lord, he had his father's eyes.

Suppressing another pang of fear, Anna trundled him along to the bathroom, hustled him through the teeth and facewash and loo routine, and then chivvied him into his clothes and downstairs.

'Ah, you're just in time,' Sarah said with a smile. 'Have you had breakfast, darling?'

'Not yet.' She felt warmth creep up her throat. They'd forgone breakfast for another chance to hold each other, and now she was torn between hunger and the sickness of anticipation.

'You need to eat,' her mother tutted. 'Sit. Drink this tea, and I'll do you scrambled eggs on toast with us. Want some bacon?'

'Go on, then,' Anna said, giving in gratefully. She needed to be mothered today, and she was going to let her mother do it. She sensed they all needed it in a way. Closing ranks, she thought, keeping fear at bay.

Thank goodness she had a busy day at work ahead of her.

'Oh, Fred, not again,' she sighed.

He staggered into her room, a blood-soaked rag pressed to his head. ''S that kerb—gets me every time,' he muttered. 'I swear they come along and raise it when I'm not lookin'. Turned my ankle and all. Blimmin' nuisance.'

'Let's have you lying down, then,' Anna said patiently, and helped him onto the couch. She eased his boots off, and a great stench poured off his feet.

'You need some new socks,' she told him, trying not to gag. She covered his feet to trap the smell, and took the soggy rag out of his hand. 'Let's have a look at your face.'

He'd opened up the same cut, of course, barely healed and not yet strong enough for another encounter with the pavement, and she washed it and infiltrated it with anaesthetic.

He was sober this time, but he still protested and complained.

'Right, while that's going numb, let's have a look at your ankle, shall we?' she suggested, and peeled back the blanket. The smell assailed her again, and she eyed his socks with concern. They were soaked, dripping with sweat, probably due in no small part to the rubber boots he always wore.

She peeled them off with her gloved hands, and then blinked in surprise. The heels and soles of both feet were covered in thick, yellowed skin, with cracks and fissures all over the soggy and clearly infected areas.

He had a condition called hyperkeratosis plantaris—roughly translated, too much skin on the soles of the feet—and because they were permanently lying in water in his rubber boots and thin socks, they never dried out and had become infected.

'You need to see a doctor,' she told him. 'Stay here, I'll see if anyone can take a look at you.'

'What 'bout that nice young doc—Carter, innit?' he said.

Her heart lurched. She'd managed to forget, for a moment.

'He's away today,' she said calmly. 'I'll see if Dr Fellows can pop in and have a look at you.'

Dr Fellows did, while she was stitching up the cut on Fred's forehead, and tutted copiously over the mess his feet were in.

'You'll need a prescription for that, something to rub on twice a day, and you'll have to get some better shoes. These rubber boots are all very well in wet weather, but you can't wear them all the time, Fred.'

'Have done for years,' he grumbled.

'Well, you can't now. What size shoe do you take?'

'Eight. Maybe seven. Depends what's in the bins.'

David Fellows rolled his eyes. 'It's illegal to go through people's rubbish, Fred. Anyway, it just so happens we've been turning out the loft and there are lots of my son's old shoes—good leather shoes that he's outgrown. I'm sure there's a pair of size eights in amongst them. I'll look them out and drop them in to your sister for you. There might be some socks and trousers as well.'

'Thank you, Doc,' Fred said, clearly touched. 'Tha's right kind of you.'

'My pleasure. It'll save you going through my dustbin. Anna, I'll do the prescription, if you could make sure he gets it?'

She nodded. 'I'll do my best. Right, Fred, that's your head sewn up again. I think there's a pair of socks in here someone left behind ages ago. Put these on, and go home and take them all off and let your feet dry out a bit. And, now, listen to me, stay away from that pavement!'

'What 'bout my prescription?' he asked.

'I'll get it for you now and drop it by on my way home for lunch—and I don't want to see you in the pub on the way past!'

She went to the chemist, popped the cream for Fred's feet in at his sister's and went home to the farm. Her mother was just dishing up soup and sandwiches, and she grabbed a bowl and plate and squeezed in.

'Smells good,' she said.

'Harry helped with the sandwiches, didn't you, darling?'

'Egg and cress?'

Her mother smiled. 'Actually, no. Chicken and salad. Harry spread the mayonnaise.'

Which explained why some were dripping with it and others bone dry. Anna didn't care. She loved him. She ate her lunch and dashed back to the surgery, covering another antenatal clinic for David in the absence of the midwife.

There was exciting news as well. 'I've just heard from Suzanna,' one of their very pregnant patients told them. 'She's had her baby—a little girl, three and an half kilos—what's that, about eight pounds?'

'Something like that,' David agreed. 'Oh, that's excellent. Everything OK?'

'Fine, I think. She was born at twelve—two hours ago. She rang just as I was leaving. I'm so jealous, I can't wait for it to all be over.'

Just then the receptionist came out, looking pink and bubbly. 'Dr Korrel's had a little girl—she just rang. Isn't that wonderful?'

'Wonderful,' they all agreed, and then the patient who'd told them dropped a bombshell.

'I don't think she wants to come back,' she said. 'She's been worrying about it for ages. I wouldn't be at all surprised if she changes her mind.'

And that would leave a vacancy, Anna thought.

A vacancy Max could fill.

Permanently?

The nerves wouldn't be held back any longer. She found it hard to concentrate, impossible to forget.

She left work, went home to her parents' and made herself busy in the kitchen.

She was alone there when Max walked in, and she dropped the knife into the sink with nerveless fingers and turned to him, searching his face for any hint.

He looked exhausted. Lines of strain were etched around his eyes, and he looked very serious.

'Hi,' she said softly. She wanted to ask, but she didn't dare.

'Can we go for a walk?' he asked.

She nodded, scrubbed her hands on the old cotton pinny and took it off, slipping her feet back into her shoes. 'Where do you want to go?'

'Anywhere. The woods?'

They walked in silence for a while, until she thought she'd die of terror. She could feel the tension radiating off him, and she just knew it had been bad news.

'I thought you weren't coming back,' she said at last, her voice shaking with the effort of self-control.

'I didn't know what to do. I've been thinking—about us, about Harry.'

'Max, stay,' she begged, turning to him and taking his hands. 'Please, don't run away again. I don't care if I have to watch you suffer. It can't be worse than not knowing what you're going through and not being there for you. Stay, and be a father to your son, and a husband to me. Marry me, Max. Stay with us, for better, for worse—for ever.'

He stared down into her eyes, his own unfathomable, and then he smiled, a shaky, emotional smile that came from his heart.

'It's all right, Annie,' he said softly. 'I'm still in remission. All the tests were clear. I've come back to ask you to marry me.'

CHAPTER TEN

ANNA stared at Max, dumbstruck.

'But—I thought—you looked so—'

'Unsure? Terrified? I didn't know if you'd say yes. I thought maybe, with this hanging over us, you'd decided you wanted out.'

'I will never want out,' she told him, her voice firm now. 'No matter what happens in the future, I will never want to leave you. Please, believe that. I know remission is only that—that there's no guarantee of a cure. It may be a temporary reprieve, it may be permanent. I realise that. But, whatever happens, however bad it gets, I'll be here. OK?'

He nodded, and his eyes filled. 'Thank you, Annie. I don't think I could leave you anyway. I was going to—if the news was bad, I promised myself I wouldn't come back, but I don't know if I would have been strong enough to stay away. I love you both too much—I need you too much.'

'Thank goodness you didn't need to put it to the test,' she said, reaching out for him. 'Come here. You've just proposed to me and you haven't even kissed me yet.'

'You haven't said yes yet,' he reminded her, a smile flickering around his mouth.

'Yes,' she said firmly. 'Now, kiss me. I've missed you. It's been the most awful day...'

Her voice cracked and she threw herself into his waiting arms. His mouth came down and met hers, hungry and passionate and needy, and she felt her knees go weak.

'I need to sit down,' she told him breathlessly when they came up for air. 'I've been running on adrenaline all day and I can't stand any more.'

He gave a heartfelt chuckle. 'You and me both, darling. How about this log?'

They sat down on the fallen tree, careless of his smart trousers and her uniform dress, and he slung his arm round her shoulder and hugged her to his side.

'I'm sorry I can't give you any guarantees,' he said softly. 'I'd love to be able to say I was definitely cured, but I can't.'

'Max, there are no guarantees. Who's to say I won't die before you of breast cancer or heart disease? Nobody ever knows. It's just the odds that change.'

He nodded. 'I suppose so.' He stroked her hair absently with his fingers, playing with the strands. She could almost hear the cogs turning. 'Where are we going to live?' he asked eventually.

'Ah. A friend of Suzanna's was in today—she's had her baby, and the friend says she doesn't think she'll want to come back.'

His hand stilled, and he turned his head and looked at her searchingly. 'Her job might come up as a permanent one?'

Anna nodded. 'It's possible—but if not, I'm sure there are other permanent jobs around—always assuming you've stopped running now and you're prepared to settle down?'

'I never wanted to run,' he told her. 'And while I was having so much treatment it wouldn't have been fair to take a permanent job, even if I could have persuaded anyone to take me on. But now—I suppose there's no reason why I couldn't.' There was wonder in his voice—wonder and hope and a positive note she'd never thought to hear.

'You could have a garden,' she told him softly.

He nodded. 'The cottage is for sale. Would you fancy living there, or would you want to stay in your house?'

'I'd like the cottage. It's a bit sad—the kitchen and bathroom could do with a bit of attention, and the garden's a wilderness—but it's in a lovely spot. Super for Harry and Felix.'

He chewed his lip thoughtfully, his face serious again. 'Um, I know it's a bit soon to think about it, perhaps, but how would you feel about having another baby?'

She stared at him in astonishment. 'But I thought the treatment—we haven't bothered to use anything. I thought it was because it was safe—that you couldn't?'

'I can't,' he said quietly. 'Well, not like that, anyway. The chemo's knocked out all my sperm-producing cells. But before the treatment, they asked me if I wanted to store any frozen sperm and…I thought…just in case one day I might be cured…I might come and find you, if you weren't married.'

'But you left me.'

'Only because I didn't think it was fair to drag you through that hell. And when they asked about the sperm bank, I didn't think of anybody else, just you. Just in case. To be honest, I thought it was a waste of time, because it wouldn't ever happen, but, yes, it is possible, if you don't mind messing about with all the technical stuff instead of doing it the fun way.'

Her heart bubbled over with happiness. 'I don't care

how it happens,' she told him. 'I didn't think we'd ever have another child, and I'd love one.'

'Would you stay at home and look after them?'

'Like a shot,' she said, laughing. 'Absolutely. And you could come home for lunch and sit outside in the garden with us and sniff roses.'

'In January?' he said drily.

'We could have a conservatory.'

He chuckled, then sighed with relief and hugged her. 'So, when are we getting married?'

'Soon,' she said firmly. 'As far as I'm concerned, we're about five years overdue for this. I'm not waiting any longer than I absolutely have to!'

'What do you think your parents will say?' he asked.

'They'll be ecstatic. What about yours? Have you told them the news?'

'Yes—I rang them on the train. I also told them I was going to ask you to marry me. They're waiting to hear, but I don't suppose they'll be surprised. My mother said you'd say yes.'

'Of course I'd say yes. I'd have said yes no matter what they'd come up with.'

'There is one bit of news,' he said, almost as an afterthought. 'They're working on a vaccine—it's designed to seek out and kill any lymphoma cells of that specific type, and once you're vaccinated it's for life. So, if any cells crop up in the future, the antibodies recognise them and blitz them. It's still undergoing trials, but if I can keep well long enough…'

He let the sentence hang, and Anna hugged him. 'That's great,' she said, letting the hope blossom inside her. 'And in the meantime,' she said with a smile, 'we've got a small boy who's desperate for a father. Shall we go and tell him?'

Max nodded. 'Yes, I think so. I think it's time. Let's tell him now.'

They went back to the farmhouse, and found Harry standing on a chair at the sink, washing his hands. George was at the table, reading the paper, a steaming mug of tea on the table beside him, and Sarah was busy at the Aga, stirring something that smelled delicious.

'Max—Anna!' Sarah said, scanning their smiling faces. 'Is it good news?' she asked hopefully, her knuckles white on the Aga rail.

Anna nodded. 'Yes—yes, it's good news. And we've got some more news,' she said, looking at Harry. 'Darling, come here.'

She dried his hands and pulled out a chair, taking him on her lap. 'Do you remember how I told you your father had to go away and leave us?'

He nodded. 'But I don't want him back now. I want Max to be my daddy,' he said, squirming off her lap and heading for his hero.

Max swallowed hard and scooped him up. 'Well, isn't that a good job, Harry?' he said. 'Because I really am your father.'

Harry looked at him thoughtfully. 'Really? My real, proper dad?'

Max nodded, and Harry grinned. Then a shadow crossed his face, and he leant back, looking up at Max. 'Are you going away again?' he asked worriedly.

'No. Never,' Max vowed, and Harry flung his arms round his neck.

'Good,' he said, and snuggled his face into his neck. 'So are you going to get married, like real mums and dads?'

They all laughed, easing the tension.

'Absolutely,' Max said. 'It's going to be the best wedding in the world.'

Nothing was ever simple, Anna thought, scanning through the racks of wedding dresses in the bridal shop on her afternoon off. From the small, quick, quiet wedding she had envisaged, it had escalated into the society wedding of the year—or, at least, that's what it felt like.

There were to be three bridesmaids—Daisy, Emily and Sophie—and three page-boys—Stephen, Thomas and Harry. There were uncles and aunts and colleagues and friends, people from university and old school friends—the list kept growing, and Anna wondered where it would all end.

From a simple meal at the local pub, the reception had grown to a champagne buffet in a marquee on the lawn at her parents' house, in the flower garden, and the church was going to be bursting at the seams.

And Max was loving every second of it.

Anna indulged him. She didn't care, so long as they were married.

She pulled out a dress and looked at it, then put it back. 'They're all so fussy,' she complained to her mother.

'How about mine?'

'Yours?'

'Yes. It's in tissue paper in the trunk in the hall. Let's go home and look.'

It was gorgeous—the softest, finest silk, in a simple style that hugged her curves and fitted as if it had been made for her.

'Oh, Anna, you look lovely,' her mother said, going pink and trying not to cry.

'You're going to be awful, aren't you?' Anna said fondly.

Sarah nodded. 'Probably. You'll just have to ignore me—put a bag over my head or something. What do you think?'

'It might mess up your hat.'

Her mother flapped her hand. 'Not the bag—the dress! What do you think of the dress?'

Anna looked in the long mirror by the front door, and nodded. 'Yes, I think you're right. It's lovely on me. Much better than all those fussy meringues and off-the-shoulder bits of fluff. Not me at all. I'm too short and dumpy.'

'You aren't dumpy!' her mother chastised. 'You're lovely. You're just not a boy.'

'Whatever. We need to get it dry-cleaned, I suppose. And what about the little bridesmaids? Do they need a similar style?'

They'd looked at so many little dresses that they couldn't remember what they'd seen. It needed another trip with the girls.

'There's the veil as well,' her mother said, rooting around in the trunk. 'Here it is.' It was the lightest lace, long enough to form a train, and in the same soft ivory as the dress.

'It's a much better colour on you than white,' her mother said.

'Because I'm a scarlet woman?' Anna offered.

'Because it's more flattering to your skin tone,' Sarah corrected. 'And you are not a scarlet woman! You're just in love. I can't say I blame you,' she added wistfully. 'He does have the most gorgeous eyes.'

Especially when he's aroused, Anna thought, smiling. They smouldered with promise.

'I can't believe this is all going to happen in just three weeks,' she said, feeling weak just at the thought of all that had to be done.

'Well, it is. The invitations have already gone out—we only have that long.'

'We could have done it quietly,' Anna pointed out.

Her mother laughed. 'No way. This is more than a marriage. It's a celebration of life—of Max's life, of Harry's, of your lives together. It's going to be a party to remember. And that reminds me, I need to ring the photographer.'

Anna went back to work the next day with a sense of relief. Normality at last, she thought. A bit of routine. A few inoculations, taking out the odd set of stitches, taking some blood—wonderful. Sanity.

Then Suzanna brought her baby in for everyone to see, and told David that she wasn't coming back. They were sitting in the garden—Suzanna, David, Anna and Max—and she announced her decision in a calm, quiet voice.

'I'm sorry to dump it on you,' she said to David, 'but I'm so happy at home with the baby, and I never thought I would be. And I hear Max is settled in well and everyone gets on, so I thought—well, as he's staying in the area, maybe he'd like it permanently.'

All eyes swung to Max, and he gave a quiet huff of laughter. 'I'd love it, but don't you have to interview and get it past some regulatory body? Quite apart from which, do you really want to take on someone with lymphoma?'

He stood up and gave them a wry smile. 'Perhaps you need time to think about it—but if the offer's there, the answer's yes.'

And he went out, leaving Suzanna open-mouthed.

'Oh, David, I'm sorry, I didn't realise. But—Anna—I thought you were getting married?'

'We are,' she said gently. 'Anyway, he's in remission, and we're keeping our fingers crossed for this new vaccine. Just in case.'

Suzanna looked back to David, her face distressed. 'I'm sorry. Perhaps I shouldn't have said anything.'

'Don't worry,' he said with a smile. 'I'd already decided to offer him the job. If he has to stop, it won't be his fault, and maybe by then you'd want to come back anyway. There's a hell of a lot of water got to go under a great many bridges before we need to worry about that one, I'm sure. Now, let me have a cuddle with that baby.'

Anna went to find Max to tell him the news. He was in his consulting room, staring blankly across the room.

'He wants you.'

'Now?'

She shook her head. 'For the job. He'd already decided to offer it to you—he was waiting to hear from Suzanna.'

He stared at her for an age, then let his breath out on a gusty sigh. 'Really? He wants me? Annie, that's wonderful!' A smile lit up his face, and he pulled her into his arms and hugged her.

'Pardon me for breaking up the happy party, but could I have a word?' David said, putting his head round the door, an indulgent smile on his face.

'Come in.'

'I'll go—I've got things to do.'

She closed the door behind her and went back to her room, tidying it in readiness for the afternoon surgery. She restocked her shelves, sorted out the ECG leads and changed the paper on the couch, then went to grab a cup of coffee.

Max and David were in the office, looking at dates and deciding when he would officially take over, while Suzanna and her baby were in the centre of a cluster of practice staff at the other end of the office.

'Excellent,' David said, straightening up and holding out his hand. 'Welcome aboard.'

It was a wonderful start to their marriage, Max thought. A real job, some kind of security, complete remission, the cottage signed and sealed. All they had to do now was get through the wedding!

It was three days away, the forecast was wonderful and life was good.

Valerie Hawkshead came to see him, her hair slowly regrowing over the incision site on the top of her skull, and she was brighter and happier than he'd ever seen her.

She was to come for regular health checks, in-between routine hospital appointments, and it was obvious that she was doing really well.

'I felt so bad,' she confessed. 'I didn't know what I was doing, who I was—anything. I was so frightened. It was easier to do nothing, to just hide. But I feel so well now, do you suppose I could go back to work?'

Max nodded thoughtfully. 'I would say so. You've got to be sensible. You shouldn't drive because of the convulsion, but that's a legal matter and nothing to do with health really. I wouldn't operate any machinery, though, just to be on the safe side, and don't strain yourself or overdo it. And no carrying heavy bags!'

'I'll let my husband do that. It's just that I'm so bored at home, and it would be lovely to sit in the shop and chat to people. I won't do a lot, I promise.' She leant forward and put her hand on his arm. 'I hear you and Anna are getting married. I think that's wonderful. I hope you'll be very happy.'

He smiled, touched by her good wishes. 'Thank you. I'm sure we will.'

He watched her go, thinking that now he had a chance for continuity, to see cases through, to make a difference. Instead of giving advice that might not be taken, dishing out pills that might have side effects he would never know about, he would be there, to follow up, to provide a better standard of care than he'd been able to in the past.

He had a future.

It might not be as long as other people's, it might not be as smooth, but it was there, and it would be happy. How could it be anything else, shared with Anna and Harry and maybe, at some time in the not-too-distant future, another baby?

Peace filled him, warming every corner of his heart, and he found himself impatient for the wedding. Anna was so busy he'd hardly seen her for days, and he'd taken to going to the farm every evening after work and entertaining Harry and the cat while the others plotted and planned.

Felix was out of the cage now, and it was agreed he'd stay with the Youngs until the cottage was sorted out. He was happy there, and there was no point taking him back to Anna's just for a few weeks.

The builders were in, tearing the kitchen and bathroom out and installing central heating and an Aga, a wicked extravagance but a wonderful focal point. The garden could wait until they had more time—perhaps next spring? Whatever.

Life was good.

*   *   *

Anna's mother straightened the veil, and kissed her. 'You look beautiful, darling,' she said emotionally. 'Oh, damn, my mascara's going to run!' She blotted and sniffed, and laughed. Giving Anna one last tweak and kiss, she went out to the waiting car and was swept off to the church.

The bridesmaids and pageboys were to follow in the next car, and then their parents took their own cars, leaving Anna and her father alone.

'You do look beautiful,' her father said gruffly. 'He's a lucky man to have found you. Many women wouldn't have given him a second chance.'

'But it wasn't his fault,' she said fairly. 'He thought he was doing the best thing for me.'

'I take it you've set him straight?'

She smiled. 'Let's put it this way, he won't make any more decisions for me without consulting me. We're going into this together. It's a partnership, and he knows that.'

'Like me and your mother. She looked beautiful in that dress, too. If you do as well as we have, you'll do all right,' he said gruffly. 'She's a good woman, your mother. I hope you're as lucky in Max as I've been in her. She's the salt of the earth, and I love her more now than I ever dreamed of.'

He looked at his watch. 'Where's that car?' he asked, unused to such soul-baring and uncomfortable with it.

Anna stifled a smile. He was a darling, the salt of the earth himself, a straightforward, honest and uncomplicated man, and she loved him dearly. She told him so, and watched the colour climb brick-red up his neck.

'You're a good girl,' he said, and blinked and looked at his watch again.

The wedding car came back, and her father helped her into it and passed her her bouquet, made from the flowers in the garden.

The wedding dress was old, the underwear and shoes were new, the garter was borrowed from Frankie and there were cornflowers in the bouquet.

She perched impatiently in the car, the short journey too long for her to endure. She wanted to be there, to marry Max before he had time to change his mind. There was a tiny, unacknowledged bit of her that was afraid he wouldn't be there, that he would have changed his mind and left without a word.

The little attendants were waiting, and picked up her veil, spaced out boy-girl-boy-girl all round the edge, and slowly, in case any of them tripped and tugged it off, they moved down the step into the church.

The organist was cued into the traditional strains of 'Here Comes the Bride', and as they turned the corner she saw Max standing near the altar rail, his shoulders squared, ramrod straight, his brother Joel beside him.

Andrew winked as she passed him, and she smiled, her face relaxing. Max was there, waiting for her, looking like a condemned man at the gallows.

Then one of the bridesmaids tripped, she felt a yank and stopped dead, and there was a little ripple of laughter through the congregation.

Max turned, and she stifled her laugh and smiled at him, straightening her veil.

His mouth relaxed, widening into a grin, and his eyes were filled with love.

He wasn't going anywhere.

Her father led her to his side, and she looked up at Max and smiled.

His gaze was steady, his eyes clear and unshuttered, and he gave her a tiny wink.

'Hello, gorgeous,' he said under his breath, and her smile lit her eyes.

She handed her bouquet to Emily, the oldest brides-maid, and smiled at Harry, so self-important in his little page-boy suit, then turned back to the vicar. It was time to marry Max—time to make her vows, the vows she'd mean from the bottom of her heart.

'Dearly beloved,' the vicar began, and she could hear her mother rummaging for a hankie already. The words flowed over her, right up until the point where Max made his vows. His voice was firm, right up to the end, and then on 'till death us do part' he faltered slightly.

'Repeat after me, please,' the vicar said. 'I, Anna Louise…'

She didn't need his help. She knew the vows, had them engraved on her heart. Without hesitation, without faltering, she said clearly, 'I, Anna Louise, take you, Max Henry Stephen, to be my lawful wedded husband, to have and to hold, from this day forward, for better, for worse, for richer, for poorer, in sickness and in health, to love and to cherish, till death us do part, according to God's holy ordinance, and thereto I plight thee my troth.'

His eyes glittered, and his fingers tightened on her hand as he slid the ring onto her finger.

'With this ring, I thee wed,' he said clearly. She didn't hear the rest of the service. She just stood there, staring into Max's incredibly beautiful eyes, and wondered how on earth she could ever love him more than she already did.

'I now pronounce you man and wife,' the vicar said. 'Those whom God hath joined together let no man put asunder. You may kiss the bride.'

And he beamed at them as Max lifted the lopsided veil from her face, laid it carefully back over the flower circlet and kissed her with all the love in his heart.

Her mother broke down and sobbed all over her father's suit, Max's mother and sister and sisters-in-law sniffed and shuffled, and Harry, his fascinated little voice clearly audible, said, 'Does this mean we're going to have a baby?'

EPILOGUE

'DARLING, you are going to have to go to the hospital.'

'Not without Max,' Anna insisted. 'He missed Harry. He's not missing this one.'

Her mother sighed and searched the ceiling for inspiration. 'You are so stubborn. You keep saying Max is stubborn, but he's not a patch on you!'

Anna sighed and paced up and down the sitting room again, pausing at the window to look out. Surely he must be home soon? She could feel the pressure of the baby, the rhythmic tightening of her womb, the steady giving way of the supporting muscles.

It wouldn't be long. Where was he?

She tried sitting, but the baby was too low, and so she stood up again.

'This is ridiculous, Anna,' her mother said firmly. 'I'm going to get your case, and you're going to get in the car and I'm going to take you to the hospital, and Max can meet us there.'

'No. Call the midwife, if you have to do something, but I'm going nowhere without Max.'

She closed her eyes and leant heavily on the back of a chair, breathing through the contraction. Please, come home, she thought desperately. I need you.

His car swung onto the drive, and he got out slowly and stretched. She sagged against the chair in relief. She was so pleased to see him!

'Max, come now, your stupid, stubborn wife is about

181

to have this baby and wouldn't go to the hospital without you!'

He slammed the car door and strode in, covering the room in two strides.

'What are you doing? Why wouldn't you go, you silly girl?'

'You missed Harry,' she said simply. 'I couldn't let you miss this one.'

He sighed and hugged her, then held her at arm's length and examined her thoughtfully.

'How far on are you? Have we got time to get to the hospital?'

She shook her head. 'No. I don't think so.'

'I'll get my bag. Sarah, call the midwife. Tell her there's no great rush, but it might be an idea if she gets here in time for the champagne.'

Anna perched on the arm of the chair and waited for him to come back with his bag.

'I don't suppose you've got a handy obstetric pack— ah. You have.' She smiled. 'What a good Boy Scout.'

'Cheeky. I must have known you'd pull a stunt like this. Come on, let's get you upstairs. Where's Harry?'

'With his grandfather,' Sarah said. 'Shall I boil kettles and things?'

Max grinned. 'Good idea. I could murder a cup of tea. Come on, petal.'

He scooped Anna up into his arms and carried her up the stairs, then paused in the bedroom. 'Stand here a minute. I'll whip the quilt off and put on a clean sheet. Don't move.'

She didn't. She stood there, calm and relaxed, and let him prepare the room. Then he stripped off her clothes, pulled a comfy old T-shirt over her head and helped her lie down.

She made herself comfortable while he went and washed his hands, then he perched on the bed beside her and grinned. 'Did you plan this, or is it just quicker than you'd realised?' he said. 'The head's almost crowning already. This baby's going to be here in a very few minutes.'

She smiled at him, utterly content now that he was home. 'It is a bit quicker, but I had a feeling...'

He shook his head and opened the obstetric pack, spread a waterproof paper sheet under her and laid out the rest of the equipment on another sterile sheet beside the bed.

'Do you want to stand, or walk, or kneel, or just lie there like that?' he asked.

She felt her womb contract again, and felt the pressure building. 'Kneel,' she said, finally losing her cool. 'Max—'

'It's all right,' he said calmly. 'I'm here.'

He locked his arms around under hers and lifted her to her knees, and they knelt on the bed, face to face, and she dropped her head against his chest and moaned softly.

Anna could hear his voice soothing her, and the strong beat of his heart under her ear, and knew she would be all right.

Max held her firmly against his chest, sensing when the baby was about to come from the change in her.

'Hold the headboard,' he instructed, moving just in time to catch the baby as it slithered furiously into the world.

Anna sagged down onto the bed, turning as she did so, and he laid the baby over the soft dome of her abdomen and sighed with relief.

'What is it?' she asked, her hands cradling it against her.

'Alive. Apart from that, I haven't a clue!' he said with a strangled laugh. He lifted the tiny child, slippery and squalling, and inspected it.

'She's a girl,' he said, and sudden, unbidden tears scalded his eyes. 'She's a girl,' he said again, laying her tenderly down and blinking the tears away, before completing the afterbirth and tidying up.

Anna pulled up the T-shirt, lifted the baby to her breast and she suckled immediately. 'Clever girl,' she murmured, and Max swallowed the huge lump in his throat and kissed her.

'You, too. Well done, darling.'

'Can I come in?'

He lifted his head and smiled at Sarah, poking her head round the door.

'I heard the baby cry—is everything all right?'

'Wonderful. Is the tea made?'

'It's brewing.' She smiled. 'Boy or girl?'

'Girl. A daughter.'

Max stood up and found a clean, soft towel, and tucked it round the baby so she didn't get cold. Then he ran downstairs, out to the garden that he loved so dearly, and picked a rose.

Just one, a beautifully scented old-fashioned white rose that was his favourite.

He was a father. Again. Annie, Harry, the baby—no name yet, but no doubt Annie would fight him to the death for her choice—a wonderful job, a cottage in the country, and to date, at least, his health.

'Thank you,' he said, to whoever was listening, and, turning, he went inside the cottage, up the stairs and back to his wife and child...

MILLS & BOON®

Makes any time special™

Mills & Boon publish 29 new titles every month. Select from...

Modern Romance™   Tender Romance™

Sensual Romance™

Medical Romance™   Historical Romance™

MAT2

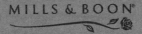

MILLS & BOON®

Medical Romance™

JUMPING TO CONCLUSIONS *by Judy Campbell*

Desperate for help in her practice, Dr Kathy MacDowell is forced to accept Dr Will Curtis, despite such bad feelings between their families. She soon realises that not only is he a good doctor, he's also deeply attractive...

FINGER ON THE PULSE *by Abigail Gordon*

Dr Leonie Marsden's first day in her new paediatric job ends with some bad news about her own health. Determined not to let down hospital manager, Adam Lockhart, she soldiers on but soon the secret forms a serious barrier between them...

THE MOST PRECIOUS GIFT *by Anne Herries*

Bachelor Doctors

Encountering old flame Megan Hastings had ignited past feelings for Dr Philip Grant. It wasn't until Megan had to face a serious illness that he realised this was the woman he wanted.

On sale 1st September 2000

0008/03a

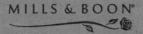

MILLS & BOON®

Medical Romance™

AN IRRESISTIBLE INVITATION *by Alison Roberts*

No. 1 of a Trilogy

When trainee GP Sophie Bennett began work at St David's Medical Centre, her attraction to her supervisor, Dr Oliver Spencer, was instantaneous. But he's made it clear he's not looking for commitment and she has a secret to hide…

THE TIME IS NOW *by Gill Sanderson*

No. 2 of a Trilogy

Anaesthetist David Kershaw was quite beautiful yet he took no notice of his looks or the impact they had on the women around him. Theatre Sister Jane Cabot realised it was entirely her own fault if she had preconceived ideas about him but could she change her mind?

FOR BEN'S SAKE *by Jennifer Taylor*

Dalverston General Hospital

When Sister Claire Shepherd discovers that the new locum A&E doctor is none other than Sean Fitzgerald, her heart misses a beat. Although she'd acted with the best of intentions, how could Claire confess to him that her son Ben was also his own?

On sale 1st September 2000

Available at most branches of WH Smith, Tesco, Martins, Borders, Easons, Volume One/James Thin and most good paperback bookshops

0008/03b

The latest triumph from
international bestselling author

Debbie Macomber

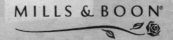
PROMISE

*Share the lives—and loves—of the
people in Promise, Texas.
A town with an interesting past
and an exciting future.*

Available from 21st July